H

BOOK ONE

THE JUDAS PLEDGE

By

Margaret Brazear

Copyright © Margaret Brazear 2017

CHAPTER ONE

Bethany first saw him on twelfth night. It was the beginning of a new year, her father had become impatient with his efforts to find a title for her to marry, and this Christmas visit to her sister was a last chance attempt to find a suitor more important than a baron, someone impoverished perhaps, who would be likely to lower himself to marry the daughter of a wealthy merchant.

He entered the banqueting hall much later than everyone else, drawing immediate attention to himself in so doing, and her sister did not seem pleased with his company.

He was very handsome; he was tall and well built and oh, so self confident. Bethany watched him as he entered and cast his eyes about the company as though he belonged there.

Julia was very perplexed when she first saw him and she looked startled as well; it was apparent she had not been expecting him.

"His Lordship, the Earl of Summerville," the steward announced him in a loud voice.

"What is he doing here?" Julia muttered crossly.

"Was he not invited?"

"Oh yes," she replied. "He is our nearest and most important neighbour. He has to be invited, but he never comes. Never."

"Well," Bethany replied unnecessarily. "He has come this time."

He seemed to have unofficially invited himself, a fact she found intriguing in this age and social class where everything has to be correctly done lest scandal should ensue.

Julia hurried off to greet this new and mysterious guest while her sister watched curiously, both her own reaction and that of her husband. Sir Geoffrey looked quite furious, as if he might challenge this newcomer, although it was doubtful he possessed the courage. Threats and innuendo were more in keeping with his custom than actual action, much less confrontation.

There was a whispered argument going on between the Earl of Summerville and Julia. It may be that he was an important neighbour and due the respect owed to such a man, but the two seemed to be on rather more familiar terms than neighbourly friendliness would allow. Who could blame her, Bethany thought, if she had been tempted by her nearest and most important neighbour. In her position, she might well have done the same.

Bethany was intrigued by this hint of intimacy between them and could not resist going closer to try to hear what they were whispering about. She never found out, because they both stopped talking abruptly on her approach.

"Allow me to present my sister, my Lord," Julia said abruptly. "Bethany, this is Lord Summerville, my neighbour."

He turned and smiled, then took Bethany's hand and kissed it.

"Delighted," he murmured. "Another lovely member of the family."

As he spoke there was a little playful grin about his mouth, a grin which reached his black eyes and made them dance with mischief. She found it difficult not to laugh, but Julia's obvious displeasure at seeing him there caused her to conceal her amusement.

Their father was a merchant dealing in fine cloth and had built up vast wealth over the years, so much in fact that he was able to maintain a grand house in London as well as a small country residence. But what he really wanted was noble blood running through the veins of his grandchildren.

He had managed to negotiate a marriage between Julia and Sir Geoffrey Winterton, the first step toward the upper classes, but now he needed to find a man of similar or higher rank for his youngest daughter.

The gentlemen of Sir Geoffrey's acquaintance were all of the same social rank as himself with the exception of a baron or two. Lord

Summerville was the first Earl to have appeared in this house, and it was clear that Bethany was not alone in finding his presence unexpected.

She had never been of the obedient disposition, never understood why a woman had to accept that her menfolk knew best and she had done nothing to encourage any of the suitors Julia had so far invited to the house. She was determined to do everything within her power to deter these poverty stricken noblemen whom her father could wine and dine and feel pleased about.

She would infinitely prefer a man of her own class, someone she could at least respect and like, if not love. If she did not achieve her goal of alienating them all, she would likely have to accept one of them. Her father was putting all his faith into these twelve days in the hope of finding someone more important.

Bethany had always known the time would come when she would have to marry and she would not be allowed to choose for herself, but the time had come too quickly and she was not yet ready to accept her fate. She wondered if she ever would be.

Her father did not really care much about the age or inclinations of a future husband, only that he was high born and could bring the family further up the social ladder, perhaps even give them access to the court. That was one commodity which could only be bought with his daughters and he still had one of those left with which to bargain. He had married her brother to a woman of his own class, but there was no title to be had in that direction so it was unimportant. Daughters were his bargaining tool and Bethany had a feeling he already knew he had wasted one of them on Sir Geoffrey, since no grandchild had yet appeared nor ever likely to, judging by the couple's obvious animosity toward each other and their separate sleeping and living arrangements. He was taking more time with his remaining commodity.

Bethany was a beautiful maiden, with dark hair and eyes, a small straight nose and round cheeks. She had a sweet voice and an easy laughter, but her one failing was that she found pretence to be almost beyond her capabilities. She had so far seen very few at this ball who appealed, but time was running out. She knew as well as her father that the older she got, the smaller the pool of suitors would be.

Her brother had at least had some say in his choice of spouse, being a man. She did not think he loved Margaret, not in a romantic sense anyway, but he was certainly fond of her as she was of him. They would do well together; they might even learn respect for each other, even if she did obey his every command and agree with his every thought. Bethany still envied them both the choices she would be denied.

She could not do much worse than Julia, surely. It pained Bethany to think of all that beauty being wasted on Sir Geoffrey, who seemed not to care one iota for his wife. But that was hardly surprising, really. He had got her dowry, now he had no real need of her since he had a younger brother who could well be an acceptable heir.

He did not seem to take much notice of any woman and Bethany often wondered if he were perhaps one of those men who were attracted to their own sex. As she looked his way, she tried to shake off the idea; she had only heard rumours about such men and she was never sure whether to believe them or not. God made men and women in order for them to procreate, to perpetuate the species, so why would he make one like that? And God did not make mistakes, which meant that such men were as likely as a unicorn.

***

Lord Summerville helped himself to mead and stood watching his neighbour's sister where she sat staring into space, her mind apparently elsewhere. He could imagine where her thoughts were taking her; Julia had told him the reason for her visit and he hoped those circumstances would work in his favour.

She was a very beautiful woman, not at all like her sister whose hair was fairer than any he had seen before or since. He never accepted Sir Geoffrey's invitations, as he could not abide the man, but he had seen this young woman when she first arrived and had been attracted to her then. He decided to have a closer look, perhaps learn her character and now as he watched her, he thought she might suit his purposes very well.

He had been looking for a wife, as he badly needed an heir to his title and estates. He had grown tired of the women in his own social circles, many of whom he had already had in his bed. Although he enjoyed them, he secretly thought of them as harlots and that was not the sort of woman he wanted as his wife.

This young girl was innocent and he could mould her to his purposes; he did not ask for much in a wife, only loyalty and companionship, and the hope of a son. He had no need of her generous dowry as he was one of the wealthiest noblemen in the country and he could be certain of her father's consent.

He was sure she had no idea he was studying her, admiring her full bosom, her slim waist, her shining dark hair. She was too involved in worrying about her future to be aware of him at all and he found that intriguing. Women were usually very much aware of him.

***

Bethany's mind was far away as she pondered her situation and wondered if there were by any chance a way out, when she felt the pressure of someone sitting down beside her.

"Lady Winterton did not tell me she had such a beautiful sister," he said.

Bethany turned her head and looked at the Earl, still curious about the real relationship between him and her sister. They had indeed seemed too familiar for mere neighbours.

"Why should she tell you anything, My Lord?" She replied. "After all, you are but a neighbour, are you not? Nothing more?"

He laughed, drawing the attention of several other guests, and she caught sight of Julia, dancing with her husband and frowning in disapproval.

"Are you always so candid?" He asked.

"I try to curb my enthusiasm, Sir, but it does not always work. Sometimes I wish there were some function of the human body which allowed us to retract words that had already been spoken, sort of grab them back while they still hung in the air." She sat back and sighed. "I will not apologise for it, My Lord."

"I should hope not. And it is Richard," he said firmly. "My name is Richard."

She was surprised at such familiarity, but she could not deny she found it somewhat pleasing.

For the first time since arriving here at Winterton House, she felt able to reveal her true self, to speak without thought of the impression she might be making. She was weary of trying to impress people of a superior social class and this Earl was unlikely to join her father's queue of suitors. That queue was growing ever shorter as time went on and this was her main concern on this last night of Christmas, not whether she would offend the sensibilities of a Lord of the manor. It was a relief to be able to talk to someone of the male persuasion without having to pretend, without having to think about every word before it left her lips.

His clothes were of the finest cloth, velvet and satin with pearls embedded for decoration. The colour was dark though, dark blue to be exact, as though he did not wish to make himself conspicuous. Many men in his position would wear bright colours and plenty of embroidery and jewels, to display their wealth and importance, like Sir Geoffrey. This man was important, and he had no need to convince anyone of it. She liked that, very much. It seemed he was also someone who did not need nor like to pretend.

His hair and eyes were almost black, his shoulders beneath his jacket were broad and she could see the muscles at his thighs beneath his clothing.

She imagined a man of his age would be married and wondered where Lady Summerville might be. Perhaps he was a widower, or perhaps he kept his own wife hidden at home whilst he liaised with that of his neighbour.

She neither knew nor cared; she only knew she was enjoying his conversation and felt relaxed for the first time in weeks.

***

The following morning brought bright sunshine streaming through the windows of her bedchamber and although there was a sharp nip of cold in the air and thick frost on the ground, Bethany was determined to walk off her fatigue from the night before. She had found it difficult to sleep, her thoughts in a whirl of indecision.

She wondered how it would be if she stole some of her mother's jewels and ran away. It was an idea she had been toying with for some time, even before her father began presenting her to various prospective husbands, but that morning was the first time she had given it serious consideration. She could perhaps travel to another city, up north somewhere where nobody knew her. She was inventive; she could easily make up a story as to why she was travelling alone. Perhaps she could pretend to have been robbed by her servants, perhaps she could pretend to be a widow looking to forget a much loved husband. She smiled at the idea. A memory sprang to mind of her father, locking away a purse in his cupboard; if she could get into that, find the money still there, she would not have to steal her mother's jewels. She was not comfortable with doing that, but to steal her father's money was a different matter. It would serve him right for forcing her into this position in the first place.

The one obstacle which really deterred her from forming a plan was that she had heard people in the north were still fiercely Catholic. Although against the law since the young King Edward took the throne, there were still some Papist factions about the country and she could expect no aid from any of them.

Was she brave enough? The world was a harsh place for a young woman alone and with no dowry and no family to support her, she would find it very difficult to make a good match. And she did want a good match. She was basically spoilt and had grown up with servants and her father's wealth ready to grant her every wish and whim.

There had been a time of religious chaos in the land after the old king's break with the Roman church. She had been told about it, about how King Henry had stripped the monasteries of all their possessions, destroyed the idols and turned the monks out on the street. Suddenly that which had been sacred was worthless, even blasphemous. But that had been twenty years ago, long before Bethany was born. She had no memory of a time when Rome had any say in the religion of England and since the accession of the young King Edward, there had been five years or more of peace and stability for Protestants.

Bethany believed they had seen an end to Papist rule. From what she had heard Catholic rule was harsh and their ideals were bizarre. Those who did not agree with them were tortured and burned alive, those like her family who did not accept the doctrine of confession, absolution, buying prayers to reduce their time in purgatory, or even paying money to touch the many relics they claimed were genuine.

She shuddered to think of it, but it was all in the past now except for some parts of the country where priests were hidden away in private houses, brought out to say mass in private chapels. It would never again be the religion of England, and that is all she knew and all that mattered.

For that Christmas, Bethany had more important things to think about, or at least she thought she did.

Bethany had been so deep in thought she did not realise just how far from the house she had wandered. She pulled her cloak tightly about her shoulders, thankful for the rabbit fur lining, then she looked up to see a huge mansion in the valley, almost hidden by the trees surrounding it. This was the sort of house she had dreams of ruling. Her father's country house, which she had believed so vast, was as a small manor house compared to this. How wonderful to be mistress of such a place, to command the homage and respect of all the people around her. Nobody then would be in a position to order her life or to decide with whom she should spend it.

She sighed despondently; she had not been born to that life and it was not going to happen so there was no earthly point in thinking about it. What she needed to think about was a way out of a marriage she did not want and could hardly bear to think about.

"Good morning, Mistress," a voice came from behind her, making her jump. "You are about early, considering the lateness of the ball last night."

"My Lord," she stammered, feeling foolish and vulnerable, neither position being one she enjoyed. "I did not expect to find anybody abroad. You live nearby?"

He smiled then indicated with his hand the huge mansion in the valley. Julia had said he was her nearest and most important neighbour, but Bethany had failed to make the connection. She just had too many other things going on in her mind, too many things more personal to her. Thinking of Sir Geoffrey's small manor house nearby, she realised why His Lordship had to be invited, even if his hosts neither wanted nor expected him to accept.

"I have wandered farther than I intended. Please forgive me for trespassing, My Lord."

"You are welcome to trespass whenever you want." He touched her arm as she turned to begin her walk back to Winterton House. "But don't run away," he said. "We should take the opportunity to get to know each other."

"Why?" Once again she wanted to grab back the word. Not very polite, given the circumstances. But he laughed.

"Why not?" He replied. "Come. You look cold and I know where we can get a hot drink and a warm fire."

He held out his hand which she took and allowed him to lead her across the frost covered meadow toward his house. She wondered briefly if she should perhaps get word to Julia as to her whereabouts, but something told her that her sister would not approve. She also knew perfectly well that to be going off with a man who was not a relative, without a chaperone, was not the behaviour one expected of a lady. It did not occur to her, however, to worry about what the Earl might think of her for this indiscretion, she just knew it was a relief to be able to not care.

Once inside and warming up with mulled wine before a roaring fire, seated on rich cushions on oak settles such as she had never seen before, she was able to remove her cloak. She could not help but cast her eyes greedily over the chamber, over the rich tapestries and ancient paintings, the oak panelling and carved ceilings. There were even rugs from the Far East covering the stone floors. At least she assumed they were from the East since she had never seen anything like it in England before. She had heard somewhere that fine rugs were made in the far eastern countries. Such things were too expensive for most people and seeing them here merely confirmed her suspicion that this man was incredibly wealthy, even wealthier than her father, perhaps even wealthier than the King himself. It was said that King Henry acquired Hampton Court from Cardinal Wolsey when he learned that the Cardinal was richer than he.

She let her glance slide towards her companion, appreciating his good looks and his confident manner, his broad shoulders and his muscular chest. She had never met anyone quite like him before, but then she had never met a nobleman before. For the first time in her life, she regretted who she was, regretted she had no right to be attracted to this man, even though she was.

"The King is not expected to live much longer," Richard said suddenly. "What do you think of that?"

She turned to look at him, startled at the way he had suddenly dropped this treacherous statement into the silence of the room.

"To speak of the death of the King is treason, My Lord," she replied quickly, lest she be accused of complying with such sentiments. "Is this some kind of trap you have led me into?"

"Not at all. I got the impression you speak whatever thoughts come into your mind and I believed it would be a topic of interest to us both. Forgive me if I am mistaken."

She was still unsure of how best to reply. She hardly knew this man and he was close to the court, and while she in no way thought herself important enough to entrap with a false question, she felt it was difficult to trust such a conversation coming from a stranger.

"You are not mistaken," she said at last. "I am just surprised, that is all. You know nothing about me. How do you know I will not betray you?"

He shrugged and smiled mischievously. "I will simply deny all knowledge of it, my dear. It is not difficult to believe that anybody would take my word over yours. Or is it?"

"You are probably right," she replied carefully. "What is your own opinion of the King's health?"

"I think it will be a good thing when the corrupt Lord Protector is ousted from his position. He has no love for the country or the people, but seeks only power."

"But if the King should die young, the throne will go to his cousin. The Duke will still be Lord Protector; I heard he will marry his son to the Lady Jane Grey."

"Jane Grey will never be queen," he replied harshly. "She has no real claim to the throne. The Scottish queen has a greater claim but the people would never accept her either. Mary Tudor will succeed, just as her father willed it."

"Mary?" She shuddered. "I hope you are wrong, Sir. She will turn England back to Rome and persecute those true to the Protestant faith. I may be young, but I have learned about the way Protestants were treated before King Henry broke with Rome, and even after. I believe Mary is a fanatic who refuses to give up the Mass, despite it being outlawed."

"And her brother allows it, so long as it is performed in private. Why do you suppose that is?"

She did not know enough about the relationship between the King and his half sister to converse on the subject and she was still afraid of saying too much. This conversation was rapidly following a dangerous path and she felt it would be a good thing to steer it toward safer ground.

"Is your lady wife here with you?" She asked, not knowing what else to say to change the course of the conversation.

He smiled.

"What makes you think I have a lady wife?"

"I suppose I just assumed that would be the case."

She got up and moved toward the window, looking out at the hundreds of acres of fields and meadows stretching as far as the eye could see. There were little cottages and farmhouses dotted about here and there, all with smoke coming from roofs. Some even had proper chimneys, an expense reserved for the wealthy. If they were part of Lord Summerville's estate, then he must be responsible for installing them, for caring for his tenants' comfort. She brought her mind back to the conversation about his wife. "Am I wrong?" She asked.

"You are indeed. I have no wife, a situation which must be remedied very soon. I am an only child and I need an heir." She turned to look at him, surprised once more by this intimate choice of topic, and her heart leapt for a second with the hope his words promised. His next words dispelled that hope. "I am told you will soon be married yourself."

She laughed bitterly.

"That is what I am told as well, My Lord," she replied cynically. "I am just not at all sure to whom my father intends to sell me."

"An odd way of putting it."

"Not at all. He wants a titled gentleman to give him a lift up the social ladder. He is wealthy; an impoverished nobleman would likely be interested, just as Sir Geoffrey bought my sister with his title. It is a barbaric system and not one with which I would ever willingly comply."

"Only the lowest classes are given the privilege of being able to marry for love, Mistress. You and I must look upon the procedure as a business arrangement, something which will benefit both parties."

"I have never heard it put like that before," she replied wistfully. "Perhaps the lower classes have the advantage over us."

"Perhaps. Just what sort of man would suit you, madam?" He asked playfully.

She looked about, returning his mischievous grin as she swept the space around her with her arms.

"This," she replied. "The owner of all this would suit nicely." She paused and laughed at her own folly. "But the owner of all this would not be in need of my dowry."

She collected her cloak from where it lay upon the settle, warming beside the fire.

"I must go," she said quickly. "Julia will be wondering where I am and I do not wish to outstay my welcome." He took her cloak from her swept it around her shoulders, then took her chin in his hand and lifted her face to his. As she looked into his eyes she felt a sudden concern for his safety, though why she did not know. She hardly knew him. "My Lord," she said. "You should have a care. I would hate to see your head on a spike on London Bridge."

"It will never happen. Mary will be Queen and when she is, all us Catholics will be able to show our faces again without having to tread carefully and curb our tongues."

She caught her breath, could only stare in disbelief. *Us Catholics,* he had said. He was playing a very dangerous game.

"You are a Catholic?"

He nodded. "You'll not give me away, will you?"

"Why are you so sure? You know nothing of me, nothing. How can you be so sure I'll not betray you?"

It was a few minutes before he replied, and when he did he was smiling with satisfaction.

"Because I am the owner of all this," he indicated the room. "You would not want to lose out on that, for the sake of a principle, now would you?"

CHAPTER TWO

How she found her way back to Winterton House would ever be a mystery. Her mind was far too full of bizarre ideas to have a clue which way she was going. At last she spotted Julia's pale blonde hair glimmering in the sunlight as she hurried across the crisp, frost covered grass to meet her sister.

"Bethany!" She called. "Where have you been? I have half the household out looking for you."

"I am sorry, Julia," Bethany replied, taking her hands as she drew close. "I went for a walk and got lost." The lie slid easily off her tongue. "I did not mean to worry anybody."

It was a tremendous effort to drag her mind away from the morning's events and concentrate her thoughts on her sister and what she was saying. Julia linked her arm through Bethany's as she turned to walk back toward the house. Her sister was not about to tell her of her encounter with the Earl, nor of his odd hint that she was still trying to get her mind around.

Of course, he was joking. He could not have meant what he said and while she told herself that, anger swelled that someone in his position should find it amusing to tease someone less fortunate. She determined to put Lord

Summerville and his strange words out of her mind and concentrate on more immediate dangers.

"Julia, what guests are we having this evening, my dear?" She asked hurriedly. "Who do you have lined up for me this time?"

"There are not many left that you have not already rejected," she replied crossly. "And I doubt you will get a second chance with any of them, no matter how much your dowry may be."

"I return to London the day after tomorrow. Perhaps Father will realise that buying a title is not as easy as it seems."

"He bought mine easily enough," she answered scornfully.

Bethany turned her gaze on her for a moment, wanting to soothe her but having no words with which to do so. She had no wish to be in Julia's position, as she was half convinced that not only was Sir Geoffrey a deviant, he could also be very cruel.

She tried to change the subject.

"I could not avoid noticing a certain animosity for your neighbour last night," she said. "What has he done to make you scowl at him so."

Julia stopped walking and stared at her for a moment, then sighed.

"You are mistaken," she said at last.

The rest of the walk back was done in silence. Bethany could not have concentrated on anything enough to have a conversation. Her thoughts refused to settle on anything; they kept flying back to her meeting with the Earl. He had as good as proposed and she was angry because she knew he had not meant it. He was playing with her, knowing how she hated the idea of having to buy a title with her life, when left to herself she would prefer to be chosen for herself, not her dowry.

Once inside Winterton House she looked around for Sir Geoffrey and finding no sign of him, decided to ask a few more questions of her sister about her most important neighbour.

"I get the impression," she began, "that you and the Earl do not see eye to eye. You did not seem to be pleased to see him last night."

"It is complicated," Julia replied sharply and with a frown. "I do not really want to discuss him. Suffice it to say he is very charming and very dangerous. You should stay away from him as much as civility will allow."

With that she went upstairs leaving Bethany to be even more intrigued than before. She wondered what she had meant by saying he was very dangerous, but it was easy to guess. Bethany had met him but twice, had one conversation with him which was far more intimate than she felt was seemly, and already she could not get him out of her mind. Her life was a muddle before this; now it was even worse.

***

Lord Summerville watched from his bedchamber as Bethany made her way across the fields towards Winterton House. He could see the house from this high viewpoint, could see Lady Winterton as she hurried forward to greet her sister and he felt a stab of remorse, a prickling of his conscience, but not enough to deter him from his intentions.

Bethany was a simple enough girl who had never been to court, never been subjected to sycophants wanting to use her to hoist their own interests in society, never been told she was better than everyone around her because at some point in the distant past, some ancestor had made a fortune or served the reigning monarch and been given a title for his efforts.

The brief conversations he had so far had with her had pleased him. He liked her sense of humour and her outlook on life, her suggestion that a title was of more importance to her father than to her. He was sure she would marry for a title, but not a title devoid of wealth. He had the means to buy her and he had the means to sculpt her to his own needs.

He would have preferred more time to know her better, to discover her principles and how strong were her religious convictions. She had been shocked to learn of his own, that was apparent, but how deep did hers go? She was surely too young and sheltered to have formed a deep conviction; new religious ideas were a fad and one which would easily be forgotten once Mary returned the country to the true faith. Given the right education on the subject, Mistress Bethany would soon see the right way.

If he did not act soon, it would be too late. Her father would marry her to any man with a title, no matter how distasteful she might find him and she could well end like her lovely sister, trapped in a loveless marriage with no hope of more. He could not let that happen.

***

That evening was to be Bethany's last chance and she was disappointed that the only gentleman who seemed vaguely interested was a hunchback. However, looks were not everything and she tried to draw him into conversation without being too forward, but he had little to say for himself and according to Sir Geoffrey, who seemed to find the whole situation highly amusing, he was not poor enough to be too concerned.

She thought again of running away, but there was little to be gained from that idea. She would never willingly face the hardship of life outside the wealth she was raised to.

The following morning she went for a walk to clear her head and tried to accept whatever fate had to offer. She was depressed and the walk in the chilly morning air did nothing to dispel her depression.

She had walked as far as Summerville Hall and stood leaning against a tree, just gazing down at it. It was an enormous house, obviously much smaller originally but more had been added and strengthened over the years. It was surrounded by formal gardens which would burst into colour when the spring came and the flowers bloomed, and beyond the gardens was farmland and rows of little cottages which she supposed belonged to the tenant farmers. There was also a small village consisting of little round cottages with thatched roofs, a small church and an inn. Beyond them were a few more buildings, probably used by tradesmen and she wondered if the village also belonged to the estate.

What sort of wife would Lord Summerville choose? What sort of high born lady would be good enough to help him rule all this? She was surprised to feel a dart of jealousy and shook herself to be rid of it.

The sound of trotting hooves made her turn, just in time to see the Earl draw rein and pull up his horse beside her. He was riding the most beautiful black stallion she had ever seen. Her mind had been so full of her own dismal future, she had quite forgotten where she was, but she could not resist stroking this lovely creature. She stood next to him to pat his black neck and mane, which position brought her head perilously close to His Lordship's calf and ankle. She felt that position a little too intimate, so she moved quickly away.

"Dare I hope you have walked all this way just to say goodbye to me?" He asked. She was getting quite used to that mischievous smile of his and wondered if he took anything seriously. "You are leaving tomorrow, are you not?"

"I am. It seems to have been a wasted trip as it happens."

"Come back to the house," he said quietly. "I have some things to say to you and it will be more comfortable there."

"What can you possibly have to say to me, except goodbye? You can do that here."

"You really are looking grim today. Please, join me. I may be in a position to bring a smile to your face."

He reached down to take her hand, to help her up in front of him.

"I am no horsewoman, My Lord," she protested. "There is little need in London and I mostly travel by carriage."

She took his hand nonetheless and was quite weakened by his strength as he pulled her up into the saddle before him.

"Have no fear," he reassured her. "Ebony will look after you. He'll not let you fall."

He patted the horse's neck fondly and gently tapped its sides with his heels while she noted that he wore no spurs. The owner of all this and an animal lover too. What more could one ask for? She said nothing on the ride across the meadow to the house. She was too busy hanging on to worry about anything during those moments, as she had a fear of heights and the horse's back seemed an awfully long way up.

She only briefly wondered what this man had to say to her. Perhaps she treasured a small hope that he would make her an offer, but it was indeed a vague one. Why should he? She could hardly suppose that he had fallen madly in love with her, should she have a romantic notion of that nature, and he certainly had no need of her dowry.

What had he meant that he might bring a smile to her face? Perhaps he knew an eligible and amiable man in need of a wife or perhaps he merely wanted to say goodbye and knew he would not be welcome at Winterton House. She still had no idea why that might be, but it was apparently so.

Possibly, he wanted to assure himself that she would keep his secret. She would, of course. She had nothing to gain by betraying him and she had already decided he was not someone she wanted as an enemy.

A servant brought wine and piled more logs on the fire. She looked at her host's handsome features and wondered how a man so very agreeable and striking could really be a papist. She would have liked to believe it was said in jest, an indication of his playful sense of humour, but she knew that was not the case.

Like any forbidden subject, it had the power to fascinate. She knew about the idols but not much else; her father would never allow discussion of the subject. His Lordship's assurances that Mary Tudor would succeed her brother meant little to Bethany because she simply did not believe them. The old King had broken with Rome, the young King had brought the country to the Protestant faith and the people would never tolerate another Catholic monarch. Catholic rule was a thing of the past and would never return. That was what her father had taught both her and her siblings and she had no reason to doubt him. That new year of 1553, none of it was of any concern to the young daughter of a wealthy merchant whose future lay uneasily in the hands of others.

Lord Summerville sat down and stretched out his long legs toward the fire before he spoke.

"Can I take it you are not eager for a marriage with any of these suitors your father has found for you?" He asked.

Bethany laughed bitterly.

"You certainly can. But I have been considering my situation all week and I can see no alternative. My father wants a title, and he does not much care who is wearing it."

"He would prefer an Earl to a Baron I think."

His words made her angry. He was toying with her again, playing with her emotions simply because he could, and she was not going to tolerate it.

"What exactly are you saying, My Lord?" She demanded. "I am getting a little tired of your innuendoes and hints. Do you know someone who would be a better prospect for me?"

He leaned forward and placed his wine goblet on a side table, dropping his hands between his knees as he spoke earnestly. Gone was the playful smile and dancing eyes; now he was deadly serious.

"I will come straight to the point then, since you seem to appreciate candour and there is little time to dissemble," he said. "I am in need of a wife. I like you; you speak your mind and seem to have opinions and ideas of your own. I have no use for a silly little mouse who agrees with everything I say and hangs off my every word."

Bethany's heart was hammering. She studied his face carefully, looking for any sign that he was teasing, having some sick joke at her expense. She could find none.

"You mean it?" He nodded. "Why?"

"Why not? You want a man who is not driven to marry you for your wealth; you want to feel you have been chosen, not tolerated. I want a woman with whom I can develop an intelligent relationship. So far, we seem to suit each other."

He picked up his goblet and began to sip the wine once more while she stared in disbelief. She expected any moment that he would begin to laugh, to tell her he was only toying with her. Could this be part of her dreams? Surely he would want a noblewoman as his countess, someone who knew how to preside over a house like this, someone who would know how to behave when presented at court?

She gazed from the window at all those chimneys on those otherwise poor cottages and knew that this was a kind and genuine man, not one who would play with her emotions. He meant it; he really, really meant it.

She could be a countess; she could be mistress of this beautiful house and these endless grounds. She could have beautiful clothes, velvet and lace, even cloth of gold, fabrics forbidden to the common people no matter how wealthy.

Excitement danced in her eyes and he studied her for a few moments, planning his next words carefully. The promises he needed to extract from her would define their future.

"There are conditions," he said at last.

"Which are?"

"Firstly, I need an heir. Whether you can provide one, it is beyond your capabilities to know but I do want your assurance that you will do nothing to interfere with the process."

She was offended and anger brought a scowl to her face.

"That would go without saying, My Lord. What do you take me for?"

"I do not know as yet," he replied. "That is why this part is so important. My main reason for marrying is to procure an heir to my estates and title. I trust you are a maid." She nodded, her cheeks heating up. "But you do understand what the process is, do you not?"

Once more he had chosen a subject too intimate for discussion and she could not honestly answer that she did know what he was talking about. She did however know that married people sometimes shared a bed, although she was unclear as to precisely what went on there.

Why was he asking her such an intimate question? Did he think perhaps she would be reluctant to do her duty in that regard?

"I think I do, My Lord," she answered quietly, her eyes firmly fixed on her clasped hands.

He gave a little sigh, almost of relief, although she could not be sure.

"Please stop calling me that. I told you, my name is Richard."

She was anxious to move past this topic of conversation lest he find even more embarrassing questions to ask.

"What else?" She said.

She was beginning to be afraid now, afraid this prize would be snatched away from her, that it would turn out to be all a beautiful dream from which she would awake, still in her chamber at Winterton House, still almost betrothed to an unknown but titled stranger.

"You might find my other conditions harder to comply with," he replied, looking at her earnestly. "I am a selfish soul. I have never been good at sharing myself with anyone and I have mistresses. I intend to keep them. I expect you, however, to be faithful to me alone." He paused and glanced at her for a reaction. "Grossly unfair, I know," he went on. "But I will insist."

He watched her for a few seconds as though deciding whether to say more.

"I confess that I am cursed with a barely controllable temper, but I do my best to keep it in check and if you honour our agreement, there will never be a need for you to see it. You will be well compensated," he said quietly. "As my wife you will have access to the court when the time comes as well as the respect of all the people who live and work here at Summerville Hall. You will meet many important people and on equal terms; you must remember that. You will not be grateful that they choose to entertain you;

you will be the Countess of Summerville and they will respect you. All my wealth will be at your disposal. I will share everything I have with you; that is my promise."

She wore a frown as she considered his words. He said no more, but instinct told her he had not finished, that he had more to say. She could tolerate his mistresses; she had no love for the man so what did it matter to her? She thought it likely she could stay faithful without too much effort, considering what she was gaining in return. Adultery was not something which appealed to her. She had forgotten the most important condition.

"Why do you spend time in proposing these things to me?" She asked him. "You need only apply to my father and he will fall at your feet."

He stared at her thoughtfully for a few moments, as though considering how much to reveal. She was sure he had secrets which were affecting his present proposals.

"Because I do not want a wife who does not want me," he replied firmly. "It is your decision whether you marry me, not your father's. We must be clear on that, whatever your reasons."

"My father will never forgive me if I refuse you."

"Should you refuse me, he will never know. I'll certainly not tell him and if he should hear of it, I shall deny it. I will not be coerced into what should be an amicable relationship and I have no use for a woman who feels so coerced."

"You seem very different from most gentlemen."

"I am different," he replied with a little smile. "I thought that was what you wanted." He paused then and his expression became serious. "One more thing," he said firmly. "You have not forgotten that I am Catholic? I shall expect my wife to follow my faith."

She drew a deep breath then; she had been right all along. This prize was about to be stolen away before she had even savoured it. How could she give up the beliefs of a lifetime? How could she persuade him he was wrong? The simple answer was that she could not, nobody could.

"I shall want you to give up your heretical beliefs," he was saying. "You will attend Mass and learn about the true faith."

She turned her back on him to stare at the gardens outside; she had no wish to look at him. What he asked of her, nay demanded of her, went against everything she had ever been taught. But the idols, the superstitions, the corruption of the Roman church was gone, finished, buried in the past where they belonged. Should she agree to this, she would never have to do anything but pretend; that should not be too difficult, despite her character. If she did not agree she would forsake all that he offered, including himself. He was an attractive man, any woman would see that, and fabulously wealthy. But was all that worth risking Hell for?

He spoke again, his eyes fixed on her straight back where she stood looking away from him.

"I will insist you stay faithful to all my conditions. You will not enjoy the consequences should you betray me."

She spun around. For the first time she felt threatened, felt a shiver of fear. He did not seem to be a violent man, he had not even raised his voice, but somehow she knew it was a threat she should fear.

This was one subject about which he was deadly serious. No more mischievous grin, no more playful smile; but what would it matter, when there would never be another Catholic monarch?

"You expect me to go against the law? That is very dangerous."

"It will not be the law for much longer. When Edward dies, Mary will be Queen and this country will be Catholic once more. I will welcome that day and I shall expect you to do the same." He reached out and took her hand, as though reassuring a frightened child. And she was frightened, but not of him. For the first time in her life, she feared the wrath of the Almighty and wondered if He would forgive. "The choice is yours," he went on. "I will leave you the rest of the day to consider it."

***

She got no sleep that night. She spent all afternoon trying to decide what she should do, when she knew very well that she should have refused without hesitation. How could she know that her failure to do so gave him hope, made him think her beliefs were a mere habit of her upbringing and perhaps he was right? If he were not, she would not even be considering his proposal, would she? Her father and brother were devout in their beliefs, her mother had no opinions which differed from those of her husband. Although her family did not know it, Bethany was far more concerned with this life than the next.

Having turned his words over in her mind all night, having compared her future prospects as they were with what was now offered, she knew her mind was made up. There was just that one condition she was still unsure of, that she should not even consider, but by the time the dawn broke she had convinced herself that she could find a way around it.

She felt sure Julia would be unhappy with either his proposal or her decision to accept it, but she was not sure why. Perhaps when she said he was dangerous, she was concerned for Bethany's virtue, afraid she might be tempted by his obvious charms. A marriage proposal made all the difference to that fear.

Bethany felt it only right to tell her sister as soon as possible. She tried again to ask her what she had against the Earl, but each time the subject was broached she only told her to stay away from him and left the room. Perhaps Julia knew his secret and was afraid Bethany would get hurt, or find herself prosecuted under the law. She need not have worried; it was not something Bethany wanted to shout about.

She was leaving that morning, returning to London, and if she was going to tell Julia, it had to be now. She was unprepared for the near hysteria which greeted the news.

"I cannot believe it!" Julia almost screamed. "He has proposed marriage to you?"

"He has. He has given me the option and has told me what to expect. I am going to Summerville Hall in a few moments to accept him."

"No, you cannot," she cried. "Please." Then she clenched her fists and looked up at the ceiling in frustration. "He is a Catholic. Did he tell you that?"

"He did as a matter of fact, but I'm surprised to find that you know it. Did he tell you?"

"It does not matter how I know, only that I do. And you will accept him despite that, is that what you are saying?"

"It is." She moved toward her sister and tried to take her hand, but Julia pulled away angrily. "Julia, he offers so much. How can I refuse him?"

"A curse on him!" She shouted. "He knows what he's doing, do you not see that? He knows you'll have no choice but to accept; he wants to test you, to see how deep your faith goes." She looked at Bethany with contempt. "And now he knows and so do I! Go! Go make your dirty bargain with the Earl, but expect no sympathy from me when you find he is not what he seems!"

She fled the room, leaving Bethany to wonder about her piety, which she had never suspected went so deep. Obviously deeper than her own, she was ashamed to admit.

But she let her go and set off across the meadows on foot. She had not lied when she said she was no rider and although she did not mind a gentle mount, she would not ride out alone. She could hardly ask Julia for a servant to accompany her, not after that display of temper and outrage.

As she walked, she still wondered if she was doing the right thing, if it was worth the risk. If anyone found out he would lose everything she was trying to gain. If that happened, it would all have been for nothing. She doubted she would still have her father's support in that event, since he would never accept a Catholic into the family, no matter what his title.

She tried to pray, to seek answers, but she felt in her heart that God would not reply. The answers she sought were so obvious and she really believed that merely to ask would damn her in God's eyes forever. Was she not supposed to believe that all Catholics were on their way to hell? And if she obeyed the Earl's conditions, would she not be on her way to hell with him? But hell seemed to be a very long way off that morning.

Bethany knew she should be ashamed. People had lost everything rather than deny their faith; Protestants had been burned alive for heresy rather than declare themselves Catholic. She was selling her soul for a title, a fortune and a handsome man, but she had privately always believed those martyrs were stupid, to suffer so for the sake of a few words. God knew what was in their hearts. Who else would know what she was really thinking but Him?

Richard was sure Mary Tudor would be next in line to the throne. That is what King Henry had declared in his own Will. The idea was frightening, but he was wrong! The people would never accept Mary Tudor, Bethany would be wealthy and titled and mistress of that beautiful mansion, and the Earl would never know her true feelings. At least, that is what she told herself as she made her way across the frosty meadow to her destiny.

She never quite made it to the house, for His Lordship was walking in the grounds and met her at the edge of the trees.

"Good morning, My Lord," she said quickly before he had a chance to speak.

"You have come to give me your answer, Mistress."

"I have. If you meant what you said, then I accept."

She was rewarded by a quick smile of pleasure and he took her hand and kissed her fingers.

"I am delighted. I shall leave for London at once," he said, turning back toward the house. "Do not let your father promise you to anyone else until I get there."

***

That afternoon found Bethany back in London, having left Winterton House as soon as she returned there after her talk with the Earl. There was no sign of Julia whilst she supervised the packing of her things, but she did appear just as she was getting into the carriage.

"Did you accept him?" She demanded.

"I did. Can you give me some valid reason why I should not?"

"Yes," she said angrily. "He is a papist. I would have thought that would be enough."

"I am sorry, Julia, but I cannot reject this opportunity."

"He will never be faithful to you. I hope you realise that."

"I do. He told me that from the beginning." Bethany looked into her eyes, hoping to find some reason her heated objections. "What is that to me?"

She shrugged and turned back to walk into the house, but Bethany heard her calling back to her.

"Then I wish you well of each other, and I wash my hands of you. You are no sister to me."

Bethany was very hurt by Julia's words and she could not see why she was making so much fuss. She could understand the religious aspect, but why should it matter so much to her? It was not she who was being asked to give up a lifetime of belief.

Bethany was resting in her bedchamber late that afternoon, trying to shut out the noise from the London streets, when she heard someone leaving the house. She looked down from her window to see the Earl emerging; he had not wasted any time in getting here.

Her father was beside himself with joy when he sent for her.

"Goodness, Bethany," he started immediately. "I know not what you have done to deserve it, but I have just accepted an offer for your hand in marriage from the Earl of Summerville! Now what do you think of that?"

She could hardly tell him what she thought of it, because she did not yet know herself. She was still arguing with her conscience, still searching her soul for an ethical way around the problem, for a way to have it both ways. Her contrary nature could not help but be tempted to tell her father that the man he had accepted for his daughter, the Earl he was so pleased about, was a hated papist. But she knew what he would do. He may have been desperate to buy a title to complete the image for which he had worked so hard, but his convictions were deep and genuine. She would find herself married to some ghastly baron or knight and her father would inform the authorities about Richard's crime. She was surprised to feel a sudden dread of putting him in danger.

Strange how she had come to think of him as Richard. The familiar name slipped easily into her thoughts, as though she had known this man all her life. She could not understand why; she only knew that very soon, she would be his countess and living in that beautiful mansion, with finery such as velvet and satin to wear. She would have fine carriages, beautiful horses and a husband who was pleasing to look upon and had promised to treat her fairly.

What more could she ask for?

CHAPTER THREE

Richard wanted an early date for the marriage. He said he was afraid to give her time to change her mind, but she suspected he had other motives, although what they were she could not guess.

He had said no more about the King's health or the unlikely accession of Mary Tudor to the throne, but she felt a sense of urgency that perhaps had something to do with the crown. Had she known then that he would fight for Mary, possibly be killed in a few short months and was anxious to conceive an heir before that happened, it would have made no difference. She was excited and her eyes were firmly fixed on the prize, the riches and the power; nothing else mattered very much.

She was longing to consult her sister about it all, but Julia was far away and there were too many preparations to be made for the wedding for her to find time to visit with her. She had declared that Bethany was no sister to her, and she wanted very much to know that she had not meant it, that she had accepted her decision.

Her father's country house was some fifteen miles from Summerville Hall and it was decided that the wedding party would leave from there. The festivities would go on for days and the house was big enough to accommodate all the guests who would come from far away. Once there, she thought Julia might have come to see her, but there was nothing. She would have to wait until the wedding day to be able to speak to her and by then it could be too late. Bethany felt sure her sister had more secrets, secrets she might never reveal.

Julia was unhappy in her own marriage and perhaps she was trying to prevent her sister from making a mistake. Sir Geoffrey had married her for her dowry, he had promised nothing more than a minor title and it seemed that was all she had received. Bethany was expecting much more from her union, and she believed she was about to marry a man who would at least have some respect for her. He said he wanted an intellectual companion, a friend as well as a wife, but perhaps, once he had his son, she would see little of him.

The wedding took place in the small parish church in the village on a bright, sunny day in April. It was very windy, as one would expect of April, but Bethany hardly noticed the weather.

She stood beside the Earl and listened intently to Cranmer's marriage service, made her vows willingly, but he seemed to be impatient for the ceremony to be over. Was he anxious to proceed to the consummation? The notion sent a quiver of fear through her body.

She was experiencing feelings she was unaccustomed to, feelings of excitement at the prospect of her future but also fear of the night to come. As she looked at the Earl, she could not help but feel a little afraid of this powerful man who had laid his wealth at her feet. And all he wanted in return was an heir. She prayed she could keep that side of the bargain; it was little enough to ask but his questions on the subject still puzzled her. Although she prayed, she felt uneasy asking God for anything after such a betrayal as this.

There was a banquet and ball that evening and it was held at her father's house, but the Earl said they would leave straight after, make the journey to Summerville Hall.

"But why?" She asked him. "The celebration will continue for days."

His dark eyes wandered over her thoughtfully, before he finally answered.

"I am uncomfortable with all these strangers," he said. "I am eager to have you to myself."

His reasons did not seem genuine to Bethany but his rank gave him the privilege of not having to explain himself. Her father would comply with any request he made, being quite agitated lest the great man should change his mind.

"Is that the truth?" She asked.

"I do not want to share you with a house full of strangers," he answered with a nod of his head. "I want us to have somewhere private to go, where there will be no raucous guests to make merry at our expense. Is that good enough for you?"

So she was to be spared the custom of their marriage bed being prepared, of the bride and groom being sealed inside for all to see, spared being washed and put to bed to await his pleasure, like some sacrificial offering. He thought it too much of an intrusion and she was relieved. It was enough of a burden to be bedded by a man who was almost a stranger, without the ritual and festivities which went with it.

At last she found a chance to speak to Julia. She came and kissed Bethany's cheek, taking her hands and squeezing them. She murmured good wishes but did not look very happy for her.

"Did I not tell you to stay away from him?" Julia asked quietly, drawing Bethany into another room. "I hope you will not live to regret this day."

"Did I have a choice?" She replied stubbornly.

"I expect you did. I can imagine he gave you that choice; I can also imagine he laid all the facts before you so that you could make an informed decision. His pride would allow nothing else."

"How do you know so much about him?"

Julia looked as though she were about to answer, but changed her mind.

"I wish you every happiness, Bethany, I really do. Just so long as you know what you are getting into, I shall pray for you. He will look after you, if that is what he has promised. He is a man who keeps his promises, of that I can assure you."

Bethany could have no idea of Julia's thoughts, that she was remembering an afternoon not very long ago. *If we do this thing, it will lead nowhere.*

"Just think, Julia," she said. "We will be living so close together. We will be able to see each other every day."

Julia smiled, but it was a remorseful little smile, a smile of regret. Then she squeezed Bethany's hands once more and seemed again as though she would speak, but at that moment Lord Summerville appeared in the doorway.

"We need to leave," he announced. "There is still much to do."

She thought she could guess his meaning, and a little thrill of apprehension shivered through her. Like most ladies, she knew little of what was expected of her on her wedding night.

He held out his hand to Bethany, bowed to Julia, and led her away. She could not fail to notice the meaningful glances exchanged between her sister and her new husband but she would not ask. Whatever had happened between them was now in the past and she was happy to leave it there.

She was soon to learn there was more to wanting privacy than he had told her, as well as why it was so important to him to return quickly to his home and it was not what she had expected.

***

Lord Summerville fought his distaste throughout the marriage service, silently contesting every word and thankful the ordeal was not a lengthy one. He had no choice but to go along with it; his bride might know he was not of her faith, but her family and guests did not and he could not afford to draw attention to himself or his ideals. Soon, he thought, soon he would be free to speak his mind on the subject, but that time was not yet.

The church was devoid of statues, the Virgin was absent as was the crucifix and His Lordship could not even tell his chosen bride that as far as he was concerned they were not yet wed nor would they be until the real service was performed. He had avoided telling her about that, and he knew it would come as a shock, but she had agreed to his terms and should be expecting something of the sort.

She did look lovely though. He watched as she walked towards him in that sparsely furnished church, her pale blue gown sparkling with tiny diamonds, her lovely face lighting up with a smile for him, her lips tempting him to taste them.

He was a little apprehensive of the night to come himself. He was afraid he might frighten her, that his desires might be too much for her, and he intended to take things very slowly, to give her time to grow used to him. He imagined it would all be a little overwhelming and after the Latin service he had planned, she would be very unsettled.

He was pleased she had agreed to the marriage, even though he knew her motives were not honourable, but he had acted impulsively in offering his hand in marriage to someone of such a different social status to his own. She would need to be taught how to behave in the presence of the Queen when the time came, she would have to learn how to live in the palace without making a fool of herself. Had he done the right thing? He hoped so.

***

It was not a long journey to Summerville Hall and during that ride, Richard held on to Bethany's hand but said nothing. Her mind was too full of the night to come to think of anything intelligent to say. She knew nothing, but she had heard whispers, tales she could scarcely believe. Her mother told her it always hurt the first time;

she had told her little else, not even what 'it' was.

Inside the house he gave their cloaks to a manservant then took her hand and led her down a flight of stairs and through a vast network of corridors which were already lit by torches on the walls. The air was damp here and she felt herself to be underground. They came to a short flight of stone steps, at the bottom of which was a huge, oak door which he opened easily, proving that it was in regular use. She gasped in horror when she found herself among shelves of stone coffins lining the walls. There were no torches here, only the one he held before them, and the shadows and shapes repelled her.

Terror gripped her. She had heard stories, tales of men who kept their wives imprisoned in cellars or chained to walls, only to be used whenever it pleased them. But she could not have been misjudged him so badly. A man who would spend vast amounts on the comfort of his tenants had to be a kind man.

She asked herself if she had stopped to consider what manner of man he was and the answer came back a resounding 'no'! She had cared about nothing but what he offered. She stopped walking, and he turned and took her arm firmly in his strong hand, pulling her forward.

"Where are we going, My Lord?" She asked cautiously.

"To our wedding," he replied.

She stopped again, more firmly this time and looked up to see him smiling tenderly. Certainly there seemed nothing devious in his expression.

"What do you mean?" She said.

"Do you imagine I can feel married after the stunted ceremony we have just gone through? Cranmer's marriage service? In English?" He shook his head slowly, but kept a firm grip on her arm. "The law might call you my wife; my church does not."

My church.

She was still bewildered, but beginning to fear that he had planned a Latin mass for their nuptials and she would be required to keep her promise after all, but it was a better alternative to the one her imagination had recently conjured up. The idea scared her and the feeling was not alleviated when they reached another short flight of stone steps, this one leading up and at the top of which was another arched oak door, just like any church door in the land, but this one was deep underground.

They emerged into a church behind the altar and inside were candles lighting up the idols which lined the walls. Standing before the couple with a smile of anticipation on his chubby little face, was a Catholic priest.

Bethany stared, her body rigid.

"This is Father O'Neil, my love," said Richard. "He is going to conduct the marriage ceremony. I'm sorry we have no guests, but you know how dangerous that would be."

She was certain that if she went through with this Roman ritual, the Good Lord would strike her dead and send her straight to hell. Her heart was hammering, her memory conjured up all the tales her father had told her about the Catholics, about the influence the priests had on the people, about the selling of absolution in return for gold. He had told of all sorts of horrific punishments meted out to anyone who did not believe one small part of their dogma.

Was she really about to pledge her soul in exchange for a grand title and a mansion?

"Why did you not warn me?" She asked hesitantly.

"Perhaps I thought you would work it out for yourself, being an intelligent woman. Perhaps I was afraid you might change your mind. Who knows? I did tell you what I was, and what I wanted from you. You cannot deny that."

No, she could not deny it. But it seemed to be just words then, not something she would ever have to actually face. She was frightened, very frightened, but not of Richard's anger, which she expected to be fierce. She was afraid for her immortal soul.

The little priest said nothing, the Earl said nothing. They both waited patiently for her to step toward the altar. Still she hesitated, although she knew perfectly well there was no way out.

She closed her eyes and began to pray silently to herself, keeping her prayers secret, trying desperately to keep her faith with God. She prayed for forgiveness, for understanding for this greatest of all sins. She got no answer.

She was quite exhausted by the end of the long and unintelligible ceremony. She did not understand one word and had no idea what she was promising, but who would know? As far as she was concerned, she was married already before the circus of the mass.

All the servants seemed to have gone to bed but there were two women waiting at the door to her bedchamber, waiting to undress her and prepare her for the marriage bed. Her new husband left her with them, and she assumed he would return when she was in the bed. She no longer feared his touch. She felt that her soul had been forcibly ripped from her flesh and nothing else seemed worthy of her fear.

God had not stricken her dead after all. She did not believe He had forgiven her, only that He had ceased to care. She had betrayed Him, so He no longer cared for her. She could not know that He had greater punishments waiting for her in her future.

She barely noticed the lavish furnishings; she had no wish to savour her acquisitions, only wondered if they were really worth the price she had already paid, the price she had yet to pay. She sat down on the huge bed with its velvet draperies and began to cry. There was no help for it, no matter what the Earl might think. She was damned, of that she had no doubt, and she had known precisely what she was doing. A fleeting image of all those minor suitors paraded through her mind and she shuddered, feeling that she could not have won no matter what her choice had been. At least by marrying one of those she would have only had a miserable life. This way she would have a miserable eternity as well.

The women servants misunderstood, and tried to soothe her.

"There is no need to be so frightened, My Lady," said the older woman reassuringly. "It'll be all right, you'll see. His Lordship is a kind man, and a handsome one."

Her words just made Bethany sob all the more, but they carried on brushing her hair and removing her clothing until she was left in nothing but her blue silk shift. They stopped abruptly when the door opened and the Earl approached the bed.

"My Lord?" One of the women said, startled.

"Leave us," he ordered.

"But My Lord," she persisted, "Her Ladyship is not ready."

He turned on her a harsh glare and Bethany watched her shrink before it.

"I said go, now. Out!"

What was this? What fresh horrors had she let herself in for? Was he planning something he did not want the servants to witness? If he was, it was no more than she deserved.

He was still fully dressed and she felt the weight of him as he sat beside her, but she could not look up. She had no idea what to say to him. He would want to know why she was crying and that she could not tell him.

But he asked no questions, only put his arm gently around her shoulders and slipped his other arm under her knees to lift her on to his lap, where he rocked her like a baby. His shirt was open, so that she felt the warmth of his chest as he held her head against it.

She felt comforted by that warmth, although she could not say she felt safe. She thought it unlikely she would ever feel safe again. Would he ever understand what she had done? Would she? Still he did not speak, but he lay down, pulled her down to lay beside him and just held her in his arms until she slept. She knew nothing else until she awoke the following morning to sunshine and birdsong.

***

It was a fine, spring day and Bethany felt a little better, though not completely recovered from the previous night's ordeal. She wondered just how often she would have to go through the rituals she had willingly accepted in exchange for her guilty soul.

She was still recovering from the shock of finding a fully functioning, Catholic church, complete with idols, Latin tracts and a Catholic priest. If anyone found that place, it would mean imprisonment for the Earl and confiscation of his property, and she had now agreed to share in that fate should he be discovered.

A female servant appeared at the bedside with a tray containing bread and cheese and a small tankard of ale. There was no sign of the Earl.

"His Lordship asked me to help you dress and to conduct you downstairs, My Lady," the woman said. She moved toward the chest at the end of the bed and brought out fine garments which Bethany had never seen before. "His Lordship also asked me to convey the message that a dressmaker will be here later this afternoon to begin your wardrobe. I trust that is all to your satisfaction, My Lady. This will suffice for now."

My Lady! It was to hear those words that she had made this bargain, but she was still not sure they were worth it.

"I have clothes," she protested.

The maidservant frowned at her as though she had spoken in a foreign tongue.

"Forgive me, My Lady," she said with a small curtsey, "but His Lordship would prefer you to dress as befits a lady of your position."

The clothes were indeed beautiful, of materials she had not been permitted to wear before. Here was velvet, cloth of gold, satin, all the fabrics she had only seen on other women. It was an aspect of her pact to which she had given little thought, but the materials did look and feel so lovely.

Once dressed, the maidservant, whose name was Nancy, held the mirror up so that her mistress could see her reflection, see how well she looked in the outfit of a countess. Unlike her sister, her hair was dark, almost as dark as Richard's and her complexion was pale. The kirtle the maid had chosen was of burgundy velvet and the colour contrasted well with her own. The shift was silk and the kirtle, embroidered with gold thread, laced up at the front.

Bethany wanted to ask who the garment belonged to. What was the Earl doing with a chest full of ladies' clothes? Did he have so many mistresses whom he needed to redress on a regular basis? He had said he had mistresses. She felt a little dart of jealousy when she thought about those mistresses and she wondered why. He was nothing to her, was he?

Nancy showed the new Lady Summerville the way to the banqueting hall where more food was laid out and where a young man sat at the table, drinking ale. He stood up quickly when she entered and she saw that he was tall, almost as tall as Richard, and that he had reddish blonde hair which shone in the sunlight. He was about sixteen years of age and she wondered who he was. He stepped forward to take her hand and kiss it.

"I am Anthony Summerville," he introduced himself. "Richard's cousin."

"Forgive me," she said. "I did not expect to find anyone here. Did you not attend the marriage celebrations at my father's house yesterday?"

"No," he replied. "I attended the other service, although you would not have seen me. Richard asked me to stay out of sight; he thought you would be more comfortable without an audience."

She said nothing, only blushed as she sat down, her heart beginning to pound once more as his words reminded her of the previous night. She had not seen him, no, but it was not because he was hiding, more because she was in a daze and had seen nothing in her haste for it to all be over and done with.

What in God's name had she done?

***

Richard was unused to having to soothe a woman's tears. Most of the females of his acquaintance were accomplished in the art of seduction and would not dream of weeping before a man unless it was part of a ruse to earn his sympathy.

He had not intended to bed his bride that night; it was late and she was distressed about the Latin mass in which he had forced her to participate. He wanted her to be relaxed and willing before he attempted to consummate the marriage, but as he held her in his arms, felt her warmth close to him, felt her soft breast through the thin silk fabric of her shift, he had been tempted to change his mind. Her tears had stopped him; as she lay beside him her tears soaked his shirt, the damp seeping through to his breast and her weeping had brought back bitter memories he would rather forget.

He rose early and went to find her a pony from the stables, remembering her fear of riding. She would have to get over that if she were to live here, as he enjoyed riding over his estate and checking on his tenants, making sure the village buildings were habitable, and he rather hoped for her company in that pursuit.

He found an ideal little mare which he kept for his visiting mistresses to ride, and led her to the rail in the stable yard, where he began to tack her up. A little smile crept over his lips; he was looking forward to showing his new countess off to his underlings.

***

After breakfast, Nancy took Bethany outside to the stables where her new husband waited with a quiet little mare for her to ride.

"I trust you slept well," he said with a smile.

"I did, My Lord, thank you."

"This little mare is very gentle, just what you need to begin your riding career. I thought we would go and visit the tenants first." He helped her up into the saddle as he spoke. "Then we can ride about the place, so you can get your bearings. There is rather a lot of it."

Bethany's heart sank. When her father or brother appeared at the homes of their tenants, on their lands, the people would almost visibly cringe and be more concerned with what he may find to find fault with than anything else. He always found something, something which would worry them into thinking they might end the day as a vagabond on the road. He said it kept them in their place, let them know what they owed to him. She had no wish to spend this day making people miserable, but she saw no way out.

Her surprise was evident when they approached a row of cottages to hear an excited voice from within: "Come, quickly! 'Tis His Lordship come to show us his new bride!"

And those words caused every cottage to open its doors and bring forth each family to come and meet His Lordship's new wife, who was astonished. They treated him like an old friend, someone they were delighted to see and as soon as he dismounted they shook his hand and wished him well. Some of the older women even hugged him, kissed his cheek as they held their arms around his waist.

He turned back to help her down, while the women curtsied and gave her their good wishes. It was a very heart warming scene and not one she had been expecting. Even more surprising was that Richard seemed to be enjoying this attention, hugging the women in return and laughing.

She remarked on this as they rode back toward the house, her on her very slow and tame little chestnut mare, he on his tall, black stallion.

"I depend on them to keep me wealthy," he said with a laugh. "And they depend on me for their livelihood and their wellbeing. The mistake made by many men in my position is to demand respect from his underlings without respecting them in return." He paused and looked at her, smiling at the surprised puzzlement in her eyes. "I am no better than them, Bethany, merely more fortunate and that is an accident of birth, not something for which I can claim credit."

There were workmen building more chimneys for more people. They were all so pleased to see them, all left their work to come and greet them, to hold the hand of the new Countess and to curtsey to her. They were all so happy for this marriage, all full of good wishes for His Lordship's future happiness.

They all loved him, that was clear, and each and every one wore a genuine smile when he appeared. There was but one man who looked surly, despite bowing and mumbling good wishes. He alone, she did not think had really meant it.

"He was not born here like the rest of them," Richard replied when she asked about him. "He came here to marry Connie when her father died. It was what she wanted at the time; she imagined herself in love with him. She knew she had no need to marry, I would have found her something useful to do, but she begged a place for him, so I gave in.

"You remember I told you only the lower classes can marry for love? Well, perhaps it is not such a blessing after all."

He stopped speaking abruptly and it seemed he would not go on, but she prompted him to finish.

"He beats her," he said at last, with a note of shame, as though the blame for that were his. "I do not like it." He paused for a moment and she could almost see him gathering strength to go on. "Still she defends him, or it would not be tolerated. Every one of these people needs my permission to do anything, to marry, to find work elsewhere, whatever it is, they must by law ask me first. Yet that same law forbids me to interfere between a husband and wife. What does it make me if I allow it to continue?"

She knew what she was going to say and wondered if she should, on this occasion, hold her tongue. But it had to be said; she could not help it. The need to voice her opinion was overpowering.

"You have broken laws before this, My Lord," she remarked, thinking of his adherence to the Catholic faith.

She was afraid of his reaction, but he only smiled. When he turned away it was to continue to tell her about his position in the couple's lives.

"He resents my interference. He tries to hide it, but is no better at pretence than you are."

His words startled her. No, she was not good at pretence, was altogether too outspoken for her own good, but she had not realised he had noticed it. He was a very observant and perceptive man, traits which she could not help but admire.

She watched his clenched jaw and angry expression as he spoke of it, and she realised all at once how fortunate she was, that he would never hurt her like that. She reached across from her mare to touch his hand and was rewarded by a quick smile.

"He has been warned, by me personally, that it will not be tolerated."

"If he has committed no crime, what can you do?" She asked. "Should you turn him out, he will take his wife with him."

He turned to her and smiled a slow smile, but did not answer her question.

"No matter," he said at last. "Let us talk of happier things."

Then he rode away, but turned in his saddle to wait for her after a short distance. She could only guess at what he had meant by that smile.

***

Bethany was beginning to feel relaxed in Richard's presence, something she had not felt before. Despite his assurances that he wanted a companion as well as a wife, he was still a stranger to her and she was unsure about his reaction to her questions.

She had been raised on tales of how evil the papists were, how they would murder everybody who did not agree with them, she rather expected them all to be angry and fierce. Richard was the first one she had ever met, and his demeanour since she met him had proved her wrong. He had been all friendliness all day so she felt comfortable in asking about the venue for the Latin ceremony.

"It is a small church in the woods," he replied, pointing toward the thick trees. "As far as anyone outside is concerned it is disused now, has been since the old King died, but it is still accessible from the house via the underground passage. Would you care to see it from the outside?"

Would she? She was unsure. She certainly did not want to see anything which would remind her of the previous night's work, but she was intrigued to know how a whole building could stay hidden.

"I would, My Lord," she replied at last.

"On one condition. You stop calling me 'My Lord'. I am not your lord, I am your husband."

"All right, husband," she replied mischievously. "Take me to the woods."

"Now that is an invitation I cannot refuse."

Once among the trees they dismounted and tied the horses to a convenient branch. The church was deep inside the woods where it could not be seen from outside and the trees here had been allowed to grow up tall and thick, in order to conceal it. Beside the church was a small cottage which looked as though it had also been disused for many years.

"Let us rest here awhile," he said as he sat down beside a huge oak tree.

He held up his hand and she took it. His grip was firm and warm, and she found it very inviting. He pulled her down to sit beside him, then leaned against the tree and took her in his arms. It was comforting, being close to him, just feeling his arm around her. But she hardly knew him and such intimacy felt wrong. It was an odd tradition that a lady would spend her unmarried life being chaperoned, never being allowed to be alone with or come into close contact with any man who was not her father or brother, then she was expected to freely surrender her most secret places to a stranger.

"It is beautiful here," she remarked. "You are very lucky to have so much."

"It has been in my family for generations. I do love the place; I will do almost anything to keep it."

"But you risk losing it every day you remain a Catholic," she said. "Supposing someone were to find out, someone who might betray you?"

"Rest assured," he said with a smile. "I am very careful whom I tell. There is but one enemy who knows, Sir Geoffrey Winterton, and he'll not tell."

"How do you know?"

"Because I know his secrets as well and they are secrets that could cost him his life."

"What secrets are they?" She asked. "Something that affects my sister?"

He smiled, shook his head, but made no reply. Instead, he tilted her face up and his lips came down on hers, kissing her hungrily, kissing her until she longed for more. She never imagined there could be so much to a kiss, a kiss that sent shivers down her spine. Is this it? She thought nervously. Is it to be here in the open? She closed her eyes as he kissed her again and began to unlace the front of her kirtle, rested his warm hand on her neck and moved down to her shoulder, taking the fabric with it.

She felt a throbbing deep inside she had never known before as she lifted one leg in an attempt to keep herself still. He slipped his hand inside her kirtle to caress her breast, then kissed her again when she gasped with pleasure.

She felt his hand inside her shift, guiding it upwards, the warmth of his fingers caressing her thighs. He bent to kiss her breasts and she felt those fingers brushing over her stomach, massaging her private places while she gasped and panted heavily.

Her fingers slipped into his shirt, flirted with the hair on his broad chest. She sensed him untying his breeches then he pushed her down onto the grass and gently parted her legs.

"I'll not hurt you," he said softly. "I promise."

She had no idea if she had intended her earlier words to be an invitation or not, but the long grass was soft and appealing and his kisses awakened feelings in her she could not know existed. When at last she felt him inside her, she knew a contentment so satisfying she could have cried with joy.

He wrapped his cloak around them both and she snuggled against him for warmth. She had not expected her marriage to be consummated in a forest clearing. She felt they had done something immoral and sinful, and perhaps they had. The church dictated the proper procedure for the consummation, as it dictated everything else, and this was most certainly not it.

His heart was hammering against her cheek and she felt him sigh contentedly.

"Why did you not do that last night?" She asked him.

"While you were crying you mean?"

"Forgive me for that, it was just..."

"I know what it was," he interrupted. "But we were both exhausted and I cannot make love to a woman who is crying, no matter what her reasons." He hugged her against him. "Besides, I have never thought it right to expect an untouched virgin to give up that jewel to a stranger. And I was a stranger, husband or no. Are you not glad we waited?"

She would never have expected a man to show such consideration, to have such perception of the feelings and fears of a woman. But his words made her feel tender toward him and she snuggled up against him.

"Your cousin," she said after a while. "He lives here with you?"

He turned to her and smiled gently.

"He lives here with *us*," he replied, with emphasis on the last word. "He is an orphan, the only son of my father's brother. My uncle and his wife died of plague some years ago when Anthony was but twelve years old. I have more or less raised him since then. He is my heir until the Lord blesses us, which He cannot do without more help from us. An early night is called for, I think."

His tone was playful, as it had been all day, and she suspected then that she had already fallen in love with him, although she tried to deny it to herself. That had not been part of the bargain, it had not been what either of them wanted. She wanted to stay aloof, to let him enjoy his mistresses and anything else he wanted, while she would not care. She could see now that was not going to happen and she wondered how hurt she would be when he went off to be with one of them. Or perhaps he would bring her back to the house, bed her right here almost in his wife's presence.

She pushed away the unwelcome idea, wishing she had never thought of it.

After supper they retired to their bedchamber, where several maidservants waited to help her undress, to fold and pack away her clothes from the day, to brush her hair and see her into bed.

Bethany had had servants like these all her life, but now she found herself embarrassed at having all these women in the chamber with them, all knowing what was going to happen, what they would do once they were alone.

She need not have worried.

"Leave us," said Richard, dismissing them all.

"My Lord?" Nancy said. "Does Her Ladyship need no help?"

"She does not," he said. "She has me. Now go."

They all gathered their things and left the chamber, while Richard closed the door behind them and turned the key. He turned back to smile at her, then moved closer and unlaced her kirtle, allowed it to drop to the floor along with her shift. She stood naked, trembling, and he pulled her toward him and kissed her as he had earlier that day, a kiss that made her feel that she was falling.

This was not how her mother told her it would be.

He lifted her into his arms and carried her to the bed, where he laid her down on the soft mattress and pulled the covers over her before he removed his own clothes.

"Have you enjoyed your day, My Lady?" He asked mischievously as he climbed into the bed beside her. "Was it worth the sacrifice?"

She could not answer that, not honestly, so she decided a flippant response was in order.

"I have not had access to your wealth as of yet, My Lord," she replied. "So I will have to delay judgement. The dressmaker tells me my new gowns will be ready in a week or two, the jewels you gave me are fabulous. I have little of which to complain so far."

He laughed, then his arm went around her just as it had the night before, but this time she was not crying, this time she was able to look up at his handsome face and tremor from the thrill of his touch.

Then he bent his head to hers and kissed her, holding her close against his bare chest so she could scarcely breathe. She found herself responding, found herself actually wanting him, wanting his touch on her body.

No, this was definitely not how her mother had told her it would be.

***

Spring was amazing at Summerville Hall. The fruit trees began to blossom, covering the landscape with beautiful colours and the leaves turned the horizon to green. She was not used to being in the countryside for this season; her father opened his country house later in the year. Here the air was fresh with cut grass and sweet scented flowers, not smells of human waste from the city.

There was just one thing clouding Bethany's horizon, that she was expected to join Richard when he attended mass at least once a day in the small, secret church. She had not been thinking when she accepted this, when she told herself she would be required to do nothing but pay lip service. She had been dazzled by the riches which were on offer; she did not understand how hard it would be to stand in that church with all its idols, to listen to the Latin chanting and she was terrified they would be discovered, that someone would find out and they would lose everything, possibly even their lives. Richard insisted all his people were loyal to him, but she would not have trusted anyone that much.

It was with a jolt that she realised she was afraid for *him*, for what would become of *him*, not for what would become of his lands and wealth. She was surprised that she cared that much, that already she would be lost without him. But that was not part of the agreement and he must never know. She would put her emotions into a little box and lock it up tight, never let him feel obliged to change any part of their bargain.

She was even more afraid for him when in May of 1553, the Lord Protector married his son, Guildford Dudley, to Lady Jane Grey, the King's cousin.

She knew it would happen, most people did. The King had never been strong and recent maladies had proven to damage his health even more; Jane was the only Protestant in line to the succession. The Duke of Northumberland wanted to maintain control over the throne and by declaring Jane Queen when the time came, he would achieve that end through his son.

Bethany was glad of the marriage. She did not want another Catholic monarch; just the ceremonies here had made her terrified she was damned, and if Mary Tudor was allowed to gain the throne, she need be very afraid of her wrath. But while she was glad, she was more and more concerned. Richard could be called to serve at the court at any time and should that happen he could easily be exposed.

That was just one more thing she had known nothing about when she accepted an Earl for a husband, that his rank put him close to the throne, whoever sat upon it. She was used to a life of relative privacy; nobody of any importance cared what a merchant's family were doing, but the King and his council wanted very much to know where the loyalties of a nobleman lay.

***

When Richard married this merchant's daughter, elevated her to the rank of countess, he had intended a few short weeks of getting to know her, of learning who she really was and showing her who he was. After that he had intended to return to the life of a single man, hoping his bride would have conceived. His urgency about the wedding had been to have her wedded and bedded before the King died, before he would give his support to Mary. The King's death and Mary's accession had been foremost in his mind then; he never imagined he would want to spend every moment with his new countess, he never guessed he would long for her company, yearn for her body as he had never done for any other woman. Even her kisses sent a tremor of anticipation through him and he was afraid now that when the time came, he would not want to leave her to go and support Mary.

He had felt her nervousness that first time, had been concerned he might frighten her and spend the remainder of their marriage having to bed a woman who did not return his desire. How delightful to be welcomed each night into her arms, into her bed and into her body, how wonderful to find she returned his passion with her own.

She made him feel like the most important man on earth; what man could resist that? But he looked in vain for signs that she was with child. He had wanted that to happen before the King died and he had to go and fight for Mary.

***

Bethany thought she could feel safe in the knowledge that if the King should die, a Protestant would still be on the throne. She was safe, but Richard attended mass every single day in his private and secret church and every time he did so, every time food was sent down to the priest who hid there, she feared for his safety.

Life was good. She blessed the day the Earl of Summerville had noticed her even though she may never get to be presented at court. Richard was waiting for Mary Tudor to ascend the throne, but it would never happen and he would not willingly attend the court of a Protestant monarch.

But that had been more important to her father than it ever was to her. She had the house, the people who treated her like their own private queen, and the most gentle, considerate and skilful lover she could possibly have wished for. Her heart still jumped when she saw him, she still thrilled to his touch just as she had the very first time. She had wanted his wealth and his title; she had never expected nor wanted his love, but now she felt sure she would not survive without him.

Each night he would send the servants away until they stopped coming at all. Each night he undressed her, which she found provocative.

"Why do you do that?" She asked him. "Why do you always send the servants away?"

"Would you rather I did not?"

"No. It is just not what I expected, not what I was told would happen."

He smiled then kissed her cheek affectionately before he responded.

"When a man goes into his bedchamber with his wife, it should be an intensely private time, not one to be shared."

***

Bethany wanted to visit her sister, had been thinking about it ever since she moved into Summerville Hall, but she could not bring herself to spend even an hour away from her new husband. He had taken this time away from his own work and she could spend time with Julia once that time was over and he went back to his estate business.

Although she had been friendly enough at the wedding, wishing Bethany well, she still wanted to clear the air between them and be sure she had regretted those words which still rang in Bethany's ears, *you are no sister of mine.*

Bethany had seen nothing of her since the wedding despite her living so close. She had sent a servant there once, with an invitation to visit, but he had been told by Sir Geoffrey that his wife was in London, visiting with her parents. It hurt to know she might still be angry about the marriage, but Bethany could not allow her sister's piety to spoil things for her. It was a shame though; they had always been so close.

Still wanting to make up with her, one day when Richard had ridden out to inspect the work on the chimneys, Bethany decided to ride over to see her. Perhaps she could finally persuade her to accept what had happened.

Although Winterton House was only a short distance, she did not feel confident as yet to ride alone, and wanted a servant to accompany her. Anthony was in the house, going over estate accounts as he often was and she wondered if he were preparing for the day he would be master here. There was so far no sign of a child, despite plentiful and vigorous attempts. Bethany worried about that, too, worried what would happen should she prove to be barren. Richard had married firstly for an heir and if she failed to give him one, she had no idea what he would do.

She had seen nothing of the mistresses he mentioned and he had not left her side long enough to have seen them behind her back. When she thought of him with another woman, she was torn by jealousy, not something she had expected. For now, he was concentrating all his efforts on conceiving an heir to his fortune and estates. Once that was done, things may well change, but it was not something she wanted to consider.

"I am going to visit my sister," she told Anthony as he looked up, hoping he would send for someone to go with her.

"I will come with you," he said quickly, rising to his feet. "Richard would not want you to confront Sir Geoffrey alone."

"If you wish," she replied, but she thought it an odd thing to say. "A servant will suffice."

He shook his head.

"No. I will come."

It seemed that he thought she might be in some sort of danger, but she could not think why. On arrival a servant showed them into the main hall where Sir Geoffrey was sitting before a dying fire. It may have been spring, but there was still a chill in the air. Seated at his feet was a handsome young man, perhaps no older than Anthony himself, and his blonde head was resting on Sir Geoffrey's knee, while the latter stroked his face lovingly.

She was shocked to realise it was true, there really were men who preferred other men and her poor sister had married one of them. It was not a myth after all.

"Good afternoon, Sir Geoffrey," Bethany said quickly, breaking the silence. She expected her words would make him start, embarrassed. She was wrong. He carried on stroking the boy's hair as he glanced up at her then smiled at Anthony by her side.

The smile was a provocative one and made her shudder. She was relieved to see that Anthony looked disgusted as he spoke.

"We have come to see your wife, Sir Geoffrey," Anthony said at once.

Geoffrey bent down and kissed the boy hard on the lips, as though he were a woman, as though it was the most natural thing in the world. Then he looked up at Bethany with a smile of contempt.

"She has gone," he said harshly. "She has been gone for weeks now. The last time you enquired, I lied. I thought then she would be back and no one need ever know, but I was wrong."

"Gone? Gone where?"

"How should I know?" He said with a shrug. "She is not with you and I have enquired of your parents. I know not who else to ask. I only know she has gone and she will not be welcome back. She has taken my jewels, the ones that have been in my family for generations. They are not hers, but she took them anyway. A thief as well as a whore."

Why would he call her a whore? Perhaps he knew something Bethany did not, perhaps something which would explain the inappropriate intimacy between her sister and her husband.

He picked up his goblet of wine from the hearth stone and carried on fondling his little friend, while she spun around and fled from the house, trembling with shock and distress.

Anthony helped her on to her pony and they rode away in silence.

"Where do you think she has gone?" she asked him. "Have you any idea? Why would she go?" She blushed then, remembering the scene they had both just witnessed. "Don't answer that. I know why, but it was a foolish thing to do. She cannot survive alone with no money, no support. Why did no one tell me?"

"I thought she may have left," Anthony said quietly. "That's why I did not want you to come alone. She has most likely sold the jewels, so she will be all right for a little while. I'm sure Richard knows people who can track her down."

She turned to him hopefully, afraid he might just be trying to make her feel better.

"Really?" She said.

"I think so. We'll ask him when we get back."

She nodded her agreement, determined to go in search of her at the first opportunity.

Her plan was put on hold indefinitely when one morning a messenger arrived on horseback asking to see Richard. The man seemed to be in a panic and Bethany ordered refreshments for him, but he refused to tell her his message; that was for His Lordship's ears only.

A few minutes after he had gone, Richard came to join his wife in their bedchamber where she sat on the bed, wondering why the messenger had been so secretive. Her heart sank when she saw he was buckling a sword at his waist. He strode across the room and took her face in his warm hands, then they dropped to her shoulders and he lifted her to her feet.

"King Edward is dead," he announced. "Jane Grey has been proclaimed Queen in London."

She knew at once why he was wearing a sword and her heart almost stopped in her chest; he had come to say goodbye.

"Mary has gathered forces at Framlingham and is even now on her way to London with an army. I will join her in Sawston where she will stay the night. There is little time, but you must promise me that you will not put yourself in any danger while I am away."

She scarcely heard his warning. Her mind was busy, thinking of how to stop him, how to keep him here and safe where he belonged. But there was no way and she knew it. She felt certain these gloriously happy weeks would never come again.

"What sort of danger?" She asked at last.

"Rely only on Anthony for news, please. It is a dangerous time and if you say the wrong thing to the wrong people, it could be construed as treason."

Treason? He could speak to her of treason while he risked his precious life for the little papist woman?

"Aren't you the one in danger of being condemned for treason?" She was shivering with fear now and did not realise she was digging her fingernails into his arms. "You are going to support Queen Jane's enemy against her. You are planning to ride to London with Mary Tudor, right into the lion's den. The next time I see you, you could be in the Tower." She reached up and kissed his lips, held her arms tightly about him, desperately trying to make him stay. She could not stop the tears which were brimming over and falling down her cheeks. "Please, Richard, do not go. I think I would die myself if I lost you."

So she had said it. She had taken those feelings out of their little box and thrown them at him, despite wanting very much to keep them safe inside, where he would never see. They had an agreement and this was not part of it.

He held her at arm's length to look down into her eyes, then smiled gently as he hugged her close. She could feel his heart beating rapidly against her cheek, could feel the shuddering sigh as he breathed in deeply.

"You really love me, don't you?" He said, but with a little puzzled frown on his brow. "I had not expected that, but you do. You really love me."

Then he returned her kiss, a kiss that went on so long she thought she would faint, a kiss that took her breath away and aroused in her that longing she had so recently discovered. And she was so afraid it would be the last kiss.

Gently, he took her arms from around his waist and pushed her away.

"Pray for me," he said swiftly, and with that he was gone while she wondered miserably if she would ever see him again.

***

When the messenger had gone, Richard sat for a moment wondering why his heart failed to sing at the news of the King's death. If only Mary had been declared Queen, as her father's Will had decreed, he would not now have to leave his wife and risk his life to fight for her.

He had waited for the Protestant boy to die, his allegiance was to Mary and until now he had longed for the day he could raise his sword in her defence, the day he could help her to return England to the Catholic church. He had looked forward with joy and excitement to the day he would ride into London at Mary Tudor's side, raise her flag before her army and claim the throne of England for the true heir and the true faith.

Since he had invited Bethany into his life, he could summon no enthusiasm to leave her, no matter what the cause.

He shook his head to clear it. He had no time for this; he would have to go, and go quickly. He took his sword from its place above the fireplace and buckled on his belt as he climbed the stairs to say goodbye to her. She waited, seated on their bed, looking more beautiful than he had ever seen her, and he could see in her eyes that she knew already what the news would be.

He could not love her; he could not afford to risk his heart. He had no intention of ever loving her, only of giving her the respect due to his countess. He did not love her! It was not possible. It was merely an infatuation from which he would soon recover once he was away from her.

But when she clung to him and begged him not to go, when he saw how much he meant to her, his resolve almost failed. He was always popular with women; he was handsome, well built and charming and with skills in the bedchamber they could find nowhere else, but he never had expected any of them to love him as this woman did.

She had kept her side of the agreement, or tried to. She had followed all his instructions on how a countess must behave so that when he finally presented her to the monarch, she would move in court circles and not disgrace him. He knew there were many amongst those circles who gossiped about his choice of bride, who condemned her as being unworthy to wear the title, but he had little use for the opinions of others.

She had stood beside him every day in his private church and said the mass as he had taught her but he knew she was uncomfortable with it, even afraid of it. She trembled with fear in that church, although she tried to hide it; she stared at the idols with terror in her eyes and she seemed no closer to embracing his beliefs.

She had paid attention to the lessons his priest gave her, but he knew the subject was of academic interest to her, nothing more. She was an intelligent woman who enjoyed learning, but she was nowhere near to believing what she was taught and now he doubted she ever would be.

He had been arrogant enough to believe her faith was unimportant and she would soon see the truth; it was a mistake he would come to regret.

Now it was too late. His duty lay with Mary and he could not afford to be distracted from that duty. And there was still no sign of an heir.

CHAPTER FOUR

Pray for me. Easy to say. When Richard left, Bethany lay on the bed and sobbed, certain she would never see him again. And she had let him see how she felt, something she swore she would never do. Now he would be concerned about her instead of concentrating on keeping himself alive. Or would he? Would he care enough about her feelings to let them detract him from his cause, the cause of putting a fanatical Catholic on the throne of England? Bethany was sure his cause would fail, and then what would become of him, what would become of them all?

She tried to comply with his request, she tried to pray. But what was she praying for? She desperately wanted to pray for his safety, even though she felt God would never heed a prayer from her. But if Richard was safe, it would mean Mary on the throne and a return to the Roman church with its idolatry and corruption. If Mary lost, Richard would die, either in battle or on the block. She could not bear either thought, but she had to choose one. Irrationally, it seemed that it was all up to her, even though she knew that was nonsense. She could not lose Richard, no matter what she had to choose in exchange.

So she waited, trying to pray, counting every minute until she would discover whether she was now a widow, or would soon be one. Because despite the fact that he had gone to fight for the Catholic cause, despite his risking his life for Mary, Bethany still did not believe she would prevail. She still did not believe the people would accept a Catholic monarch, and that meant the man she had fallen so desperately in love with, would die, and her future with him. There would never be another and she would grieve for him for the rest of her days.

And she believed she understood now his urgency about the marriage. He wanted an heir before he left to fight for Mary, before he was killed fighting for Mary. She had failed him in that and now she was so afraid he would never come back to forgive her.

The messenger did not get there before the torches were lit across the country. Bethany had not really seen this display before, or at least not noticed it. The first torch she saw was in their own village, then she looked farther into the distance to see the flames getting smaller and smaller as they moved away to other parts of the country, all the way from London, proclaiming the victory of Mary.

She finally forced herself to do what she had half hoped she would never have to. She made her way down those stairs and along those tapestry covered passages until she reached the huge, arch shaped oak door that led into the old church. She stood staring at the door for a long time, her heart hammering as she prayed for forgiveness. The first time she had been here, Richard was holding her hand and she had not known what was on the other side. She had never willingly come to this place, always with him, always because it was what he expected, what she had promised him. This time was different, this time she was entering this iniquitous place of her own free will, only to find out if she could ever feel safe in such a place. Her prayers had been answered, Mary had won and Richard was safe, she would have to enter this place and others like it and she wanted to know if she could do that without fearing the wrath of God.

At last, she took a deep breath to still her racing heart and turned the iron handle. She was surprised to find the candles lit and the little priest kneeling at the altar. He looked up sharply when she entered, then smiled and rose to his feet, reaching out a welcoming hand.

"My lady," he greeted her. "Welcome."

And so it began. Father O'Neil led her through long and complicated instructions, about the Catholic faith, about the belief system and dogma that she had accepted so flippantly. Then came a Latin service, and when she left the church, she felt she had made a pact with Satan which could never be forgiven. And she did not do this for riches and position, for a title. She did it for the love of one man. That had not been her intention when she accepted his treacherous bargain, had it? She was going to brazenly forgive his infidelities, she would accept his Papist ideals, because of the wealth and power he had to offer her. Now none of those things mattered any more; she would live in a wooden hut with him. She had known exactly what she wanted; she had known exactly what she was doing.

She sought out Anthony for advice, as although he was only young, he was wise and knew more about what went on than she. Nobody would think to tell a woman, even if she were a countess.

"I doubt he will be home yet," he answered her enquiry. "He will stay at court until the coronation. He will want you to join him I should think, but we best wait for word."

"But Mary has won," she said. "Why does he need to stay there?"

Anthony was thoughtful for a moment before he finally answered.

"I think perhaps Richard told you little of what his role would be when Mary succeeded to the throne."

"His role?" Bethany repeated. "I'm not sure what you mean. He said he would support her and he has done so. Why can he not now come home?"

"He has always been highly thought of by Mary," Anthony replied. "She has depended on him for advice in the past and now she is Queen, doubtless that dependency will increase. She will need him by her side."

She made no reply, only left the house to walk in the grounds and think about his words. She had never expected this, had not realised that he would have an important position at court. He had not once set foot in the palace while young Edward was King. This would mean she would have to be with him at court, have to suffer the presence of the mad fanatic every day.

She could only pray she could keep up the pretence in the presence of the Queen. She would have to wait until Richard sent for her to find out just where her future lay, what he intended for her.

So wait she did, but not with patience. She was anxious to learn what changes this new Queen would make and how soon she would begin to persecute the Protestants. Anthony said she had promised not to force people to follow her religious beliefs, but Bethany found that hard to believe. One of the tenets of the papist dogma was that they shalt not suffer a heretic to live.

It was only two or three weeks before the men began to return from London, bringing with them word from Lord Summerville. He wanted his wife to join him, he wanted to present her to the Queen. He wanted her at the coronation, but he told her to wait as he would have no time for her in London.

She was despondent, but knew he was right. He was close to Queen Mary and she had no wish to meet her before she absolutely had to. From the years of stories she had been told, she imagined her as an evil witch, laughing as she watched the heretics burn.

Bethany would spend the time exploring the mansion in which she now lived, in which she could so easily get lost. There were many rooms, many portraits along galleries and in chambers that were never used. The entire east wing was closed up. Houses like this were built so the reigning monarch and all his court could visit and stay in comfort. Sometimes those visits had left a family penniless, but there was nothing to be done about them. Since the death of King Henry there had been no royal visits to Summerville Hall, as the family had not been in favour with the young King Edward. Bethany suddenly realised this would all change now, that Mary might well descend upon them with all her court. Her immediate thought was of where she could hide, where she could escape should that happen, but she did not think Richard would allow it. She had made a promise and her place was at his side, no matter how difficult that turned out to be.

She found her way to the attics, which she had not known existed. There was a flight of stairs and a small door which led into a dusty room full of paintings and cobwebs. She crossed to the window and rubbed at the grime with her sleeve to see the view across the fields. Winterton House looked tiny in the distance, but the sight of it brought her mind back to Julia. She could hardly wait to begin her search for her, but she had to stay here, stay where she could be summoned if needed. Julia had chosen to go; surely if she were in any trouble she would send word.

The paintings which were piled against the walls were very dirty, so much so that it was difficult to make out the detail. A lot were landscapes, there was one of Summerville Hall itself, although not a very good one. She supposed that was the reason it was hidden away here. As to the others, there were so many of them. There was only so much wall space to be had.

She pulled one away to find herself looking into the very pale face of a pretty young girl with auburn hair and green eyes. Her green gown was of the finest velvet and she wore a necklace of pearls, but her expression was sad. She took it to the window to try to get some more light on that face, but it was impossibly dirty, so she carried it out of the attic and along the corridor to her own chamber. It was a very big painting and far too heavy for her to take further.

In a chest she found a cloth that had been used to polish some boots and she wiped away the grime with that. Clean, the girl in the portrait looked even sadder, and Bethany wondered who she was. She could barely make out the writing engraved at the bottom of the frame, so she spat on the cloth and scrubbed away at it until it became clear.

'Rosemary, fourth Countess of Summerville' it read.

Bethany just stared for a moment, thinking she must have read it wrongly. But no, it definitely declared this to be the fourth Countess of Summerville. But was she not the fourth Countess? It is what she believed and she saw no reason to doubt either Richard's word or her own senses. On the other hand, nobody had actually told her that; she had just assumed, knowing her husband was the fourth Earl. Nobody had lied, had they? Merely not corrected an assumption they may not have even know she had made.

She leaned the picture against the wall beneath the window and stared at it. The title could only mean one thing that she could think of: Richard had been married before, which made a lot more sense, considering his age and his social position. But why had he not told her? She recalled asking him about a wife and he had only replied that he did not have one, not that she was dead, as Bethany could only assume she was. It would seem a more natural response, would it not? She also wondered why her portrait was hidden in the attic to rot away beneath the dust and the spiders' webs.

Was it possible he had hidden it there himself when she agreed to marry him? Perhaps he thought it might cause her distress to have it on display. But no; she could see that the grime which covered her lovely face was the accumulation of a lot longer than the few months since their marriage. Rosemary had been consigned to the dusty depths of the attic long before her successor came along.

Bethany went downstairs in the hope that Anthony would have a different explanation. She waited until he had finished giving orders to the steward and had turned to smile at her.

"Who is Rosemary?" She asked without preamble.

He drew himself up sharply and took a deep breath.

"How did you find out about her?" He asked.

"I found her portrait. If she is the fourth Countess, who am I? And where is she?"

"She is dead," he replied. "She died of plague at the same time as my parents."

"But who was she? Why did Richard not tell me he had been married before?"

Anthony did not reply for a few moments, as he thought about his answer, not wanting to say the wrong thing.

"You had best save that question until Richard returns," he said at last. "It is not a subject I know enough about. It is his business and up to him to tell you."

With that he left her sitting beside the window, gazing out thoughtfully at the summer landscape. The church was visible now through the trees; there was no longer any reason to keep it hidden, so a clearing had been made. Staring across at it, she noticed that the cottage next to the church remained hidden. There had been no need to reveal its whereabouts when the church was uncovered. She needed a walk, she needed to feel the sun on her face and ponder her discovery. She would not feel secure until she knew the truth about Rosemary, until she knew why he had kept this secret from her.

As she walked she thought about the pretty face in the portrait and tried to imagine her with Richard, tried to imagine her in his bed, in his arms, making love to him, and she thought she knew why he had never spoken of his first wife. Obviously the memory was too painful; he must have loved her very much and the notion made Bethany's heart twist with jealousy. What had Rosemary had which she did not? Why did he love her so much, but did not love Bethany? She wished she had never discovered that painting.

After a walk of some twenty minutes across the meadow she was hot and grateful for the coolness of the thick foliage when she finally stepped into the woods. The little cottage was deeper inside, but she could just make out the wattle and daub walls. This place was old, very old and she wondered what it was doing here, what it had been built for. It would be the right position for the priest's home, yet it seemed too small and humble for such a man.

It didn't look as though anyone had been inside for many years, but the door was not locked so she opened it carefully and went in. The door creaked a lot, making her wary of arousing some entity of the woods. It was furnished very sparsely, but it was clean, not dusty like somewhere that had been disused for years. She glanced around, looking into the small space. The fireplace was a circle of stones in the centre of the small room and directly above was a hole in the ceiling to release the smoke. There was a wooden bar across which held a huge cauldron and the ashes beneath it were still warm. Someone had been living here, but there was no sign of any clothing or personal items. It was as if someone had moved on, perhaps sensing she would be looking inside, or someone would.

She was just coming out of the front door when she saw the little priest emerging from the church. He smiled at her, just as he had the first time she had encountered him, and walked quickly toward her.

"Can I help you with anything, My Lady?" He said pleasantly. "If you wish me to hear your confession, it is no trouble to open the church again."

Confession? She shuddered at the very idea, but realised it was another aspect of the faith she had not taken into account. She had managed to avoid it so far, since it was an intensely private thing and not something Richard would enquire about, either to her or to Father O'Neil. The very idea of exposing her private thoughts to anyone, much less a celibate priest, was abhorrent to her.

She wondered what sort of absolution he would offer if she confessed to him her almost unbearable guilt at participating in Latin masses, that she felt she was giving a little more of her soul to Satan every time she did so.

"No, Father," she replied quickly. "Nothing of the sort. I was just wondering who lived in the little cottage." Then it dawned on her and she wondered why she had not realised before. "Of course, I expect you have been living there yourself."

"I have indeed, My Lady. But now the true faith will be restored, His Lordship has invited me to live at Summerville Hall."

When had he done that? He could not have known Mary would win, but still it must have been arranged before he left.

"When we married," she suddenly asked the priest, "did His Lordship tell you he was a widower?"

"Of course, My Lady," Father O'Neil replied.

Of course he had. He would not lie to a priest, but he had no hesitation in concealing it from her!

The next day a messenger arrived from London. Richard was ready for her to join him at Court, the coronation was set for October and he wanted her to be there. The Queen was very family minded and was eager to meet the wife of one of her most trusted and loyal courtiers.

She was not looking forward to that, but her heart sang to know she would soon be with Richard. She suspected she had at last conceived, but while she longed to see his joy when she told him, she wanted to keep it to herself until she was absolutely certain. It must have happened that last night, before he went away, as though God knew he would not be coming back. But he had come back, so what did that mean? Could it be that God really was on Mary's side?

While servants packed her things two gentlemen arrived to escort her to Court. She felt very important, just as she had wanted, but she also felt their happy solitude was over. Now that Richard was an important figure at Court, would they ever again share that quiet companionship which had meant so much to her?

***

It was just a week until the date set for the coronation. Gathering support for Mary had been comparatively easy and took little time and little bloodshed, thank the Lord. Mary and her army were welcomed in London, as Richard suspected would be the case; she was the rightful heir and the people knew that.

Now most of the work was done, most of the arrangements were in place and he would have to send for Bethany to join him. He had hoped that being away from her would cure him of what he believed to be an infatuation, but it had not worked that way. He had missed her terribly; his sleep was filled with dreams of her, of her lovely face, of her sensual body and he did not like it.

He knew she had fallen in love with him, knew by the frantic way she had begged him to stay with her, and his fear was that she would be badly hurt. He wanted to make her think less of him, wanted to push her away so she would not be hurt when he gave his allegiance to the Queen, when he put that Queen before his wife. He thought about her reaction to the Catholic services in his church and he dreaded having to present her to Mary. Pretence was not Bethany's strength, a fact which had endeared her to him, but now pretence might be the most important thing she had ever had to do.

He needed to push her away, for her own sake. He tried to be angry that she had not yet conceived a child; if he were angry it would be easier for him to show her his dark side, but he was a fair man and it seemed unfair to blame her for something which was of no fault of hers. Still, it was something to think about.

***

On reaching the city, Bethany was conveyed to Whitehall Palace and taken to a suite of rooms on the first floor. Her mind was full of questions about Richard's first wife, about Julia and how to find her; there was so much she wanted to discuss with him. Her mind was so busy and she was so excited to know she would soon be seeing him again, she hardly noticed the magnificent building. When she stepped inside the chamber and saw him sitting at the table, everything else flew out of her mind and her heart leapt into her throat.

He stood up from the table where he had been writing and smiled as he walked swiftly toward her, his hand out ready to take hers. She ignored his hand and fell into his arms, determined that any thought of Rosemary would not spoilt this moment.

"I have missed you so much," she murmured between kisses. "I could not have spent another day apart from you."

He held her close and his kisses were hungry, making her throb with longing for him, and she had no control over her tears.

He took her face between his hands and looked down with a concerned frown.

"Why the tears? Are you not happy to be here?"

"I am. I know not why I am crying, probably because it is so good to feel your arms around me once more."

"You have had a long journey. Refreshments will be here soon, then we can rest for a little while. There is a lot to prepare before the coronation."

"Will we be able to go home afterwards?" She asked impulsively. "Or will we have to stay here?"

He frowned and gripped her shoulders as he held her away from him.

"It will be the Queen's decision, Bethany," he replied. "Not mine. Besides, I thought that was what you wanted, to be presented at Court, to be rich and important."

Was he teasing? His expression said not but she was unsure and she did not like his tone one bit. Something had changed since he went away; he had never spoken to her like this before. She remembered he had spoken of mistresses; how had she forgotten that? Now she wondered if her arrival had interrupted his pleasure. She caught back a sob and tried to pretend she had not noticed his cynical tone.

"But you cannot spare the time away from Summerville Hall," she argued. "People there need you."

"Anthony can run the estate," he replied then he looked at her thoughtfully before he spoke again. "It seems he may have to get used to it after all, does it not?"

She knew what he was referring to, and she could scarcely believe she was hearing such harsh words from him. But still there was no tone of anger, only disappointment and that tone hurt more than anything.

She ought to tell him now, tell him she was likely with child, but a stubborn part of her nature refused.

"There is still time," she replied, but she sounded submissive even to her own ears and that was not an impression she wanted to give to anyone. "Or are you anxious to get back to your mistresses, My Lord?"

He looked startled, then he pulled her toward him and held her close.

"Forgive me," he said. "I am tired. It has been a great strain and as you say, we still have lots of time."

***

Being presented to the Queen was terrifying. All her life Bethany had heard how fanatical she was, and she felt irrationally that those huge, staring eyes of hers were looking right into her soul, knew how she felt. The presentation took place in the royal apartments in the Tower, where Mary would lodge until her coronation. She did not say much, for which Bethany was thankful.

She wanted so much to do this right, she did not want to let Richard down and this meant so much to him; she hoped she was not losing the struggle to hide her distaste.

When the Queen held out her hand to be kissed, Bethany hesitated, looking at the wrinkled fingers with their gemstone rings before she finally complied. It was a difficult thing to do and she could feel Richard's eyes upon her, watching her, scrutinising her every move. She glanced at him and saw that his jaw was clenched, his hands bunched into fists and knew she was seeing a glimpse of that temper he had warned her about.

There were hints of a permanent position at court but she did not think she could be near this woman every day of her life without displaying her dislike. And that would be the end; Richard was already angry with her. He would tolerate no more.

Bethany believed this frail looking woman would be the cause of reviving the barbarous punishment of burning people alive for heresy. She could be the death of her entire family and could never be made to see another's viewpoint on the subject of religion. She had heard that Mary refused to even read a letter from a Protestant, lest the very words taint her. The worst thing was knowing that her husband would be helping the Queen to bring back those barbaric laws. Yet she loved him, she loved him more than anything in the world.

Her family had disowned her on learning of her husband's religious leanings, but they were still her kin and she felt a deep hatred for this little woman which she found almost impossible to conceal. How was she expected to be close to her on a daily basis without that hatred revealing itself? Once again she was betraying her promises to Richard. He had assured her that Mary would be Queen, he had been very certain, but she had not listened. She had not believed him, had thought it was just wishful thinking on his part and now she was forced to face her.

It would have made no difference if she had accepted his word; she had no idea then what it would mean to her because she had no idea how the nobility lived. He had failed to tell her that he would be living in the palace and giving his advice to the Catholic Queen.

Bethany had not so far enjoyed her time in London and could only hope it may soon be over, that Richard would agree to return to Suffolk. The coronation was but a few days away.

The image of Rosemary still hovered at the back of her mind, but she felt she should wait until they were home again to ask about her. Here he had too much to do, he was different and after witnessing his anger when she met the Queen, she felt it would take more courage than at home in familiar surroundings. Had he wanted to talk about her, he would surely have mentioned her, not ignored her existence and hidden her portrait away where no one could see it.

Although Mary had been given the support she needed to reclaim her throne, Bethany was still not convinced she was a popular choice. It seemed the people wanted a daughter of bluff

King Hal on the throne, not a distant cousin with little claim, but she did not expect the celebrations which took place. There was cheering and waving from all the people, everyone was dancing with joy. Everyone, it seemed, except the new Lady Summerville.

Bethany was exhausted at the end of the day. She rode with other ladies behind the royal entourage and Richard rode in front with other courtiers and close to the Queen. Behind her, in their own carriage, rode her sister, Elizabeth, with Anne of Cleves, the woman who was too ugly for King Henry to bed. She didn't look in any way unattractive to Bethany; in fact she seemed to be equally as lovely as his other queens. Considering his subsequent acts, Anne had indeed had a lucky escape.

Bethany was still not much of a horsewoman and the muscles in her back were unused to so many hours in the saddle, but she had refused to share a carriage. She did not want to have to pretend joy at this occasion; she was better on horseback where she would need talk to no one. By the time they were able to retire to bed that night, her back was stiff and sore.

Richard lay beside her and massaged her back until it felt a little better, the feel of his strong fingers as they soothed her muscles, arousing her. On several nights since her arrival in London she had been asleep when he retired for the night and she felt he was trying to avoid her.

She told herself it was her imagination; she had missed her nights with him so much, she could not bear the idea that he did not share her feelings.

She turned over and looked up at him nervously. He was still the same man who had ridden off to fight his cause. Why then did she suddenly fear him?

He kissed her, then slipped his hand inside her shift to gently hold her breast. Did he know he had only to touch her to drive all other thoughts racing from her mind? But his lovemaking that night was different, subdued and distant somehow, as though he was trying to spare himself some private pain.

***

Richard knew it would be a disaster as soon he saw his wife's first reaction to the Queen. She tried hard to hide it, but the dislike was there. He could see it because he knew her so well; he could only hope others would not see it.

Even his attempt to make her think less of him had ended in a jolt of pain he had not expected. Why was that? He thought to embarrass her, to make her feel inadequate and perhaps blame him for that.

But she fought back with words which stung. Why did her mention of his mistresses hurt him? Was it because he could not bear to have her think ill of him? But that had been his intention all along. Once he knew how it would really feel for her to think badly of him, he decided it was not such a good idea after all.

He was only trying to push her away so she did not get hurt. He had never really expected the meeting with the Queen to work out well, and now Mary wanted his wife as a Lady in waiting and he would have to find some way to refuse her. Bethany would have to be sent home while he stayed here in London, and that was going to cause her pain because he had allowed her to fall in love with him.

He blamed himself for that. He had been too kind to her, that was the problem. He could easily have been dispassionate, given her no consideration and shown her no affection, but it had never occurred to him; he was enjoying her too much. Now it was too late.

The first night she arrived in London, he could not wait to undress her and feel that gorgeous body next to his again, to bury himself inside her and love her once more. His plan to push her away would never work if he could not keep his own emotions under control.

He had been so angry at the meeting between the Queen and his countess, and Bethany had noticed that. He was not angry with her, he was angry with himself for not realising what would happen. But he would let her go on thinking she had enraged him; it might make things easier for them both.

***

The processions went on for two days with the coronation at the end. Once more he massaged her back, once more he made love to her.

"Can we return to Summerville now?" She asked.

He shook his head.

"No, Bethany. I already told you; the Queen needs me here."

She was silent for a few seconds, then she moved across the bed and put her arms around his waist, his flesh warm against hers.

"Very well," she murmured. "How long will we have to stay?"

He hugged her against him and kissed the top of her head before he answered and his words cut through her like a sharp blade.

"I think I shall escort you home to Summerville tomorrow," he said quietly. "But I cannot stay. You will be better off at home."

She swallowed hard to trap an escaping sob.

"Why would you send me away? Do you not want me here?"

"No." His expression had not changed, his tone was still gentle, but there was no doubt that he meant it. "You are not safe here, Bethany. I saw how you greeted the Queen; one day she will see it too. This is a dangerous place for you."

"Please," she argued. "I can do better, really I can."

"I am sorry. I will not take the chance, not with your life."

She lay awake that night feeling that her world had ended, that the few months of bliss were over and that bliss would never return. He was right about it not being safe, he was right that she found it hard to conceal her hatred of the Queen, but she felt sure that was only an excuse to send her home. She had let him down; she had not given him the son for which he had married and she could not even pretend to be a good Catholic. They were the two most important things he had wanted from her, and she had failed in them both. Any idea she might have nourished that he felt the same for her as she did for him, faded away with the realisation that she was nothing more than a breeding vessel.

He would stay at court, she would not see him and he would have his mistresses. All she would have would be memories of a passion so intense she would have killed for one more night with him.

***

Bethany concentrated her thoughts on the scenery as they rode home in the carriage. She had nothing to say to Richard, nothing that would change his mind and make him stay, and there was an awkwardness between them that had never been there before, not even at the very beginning when they were strangers. She did not know where this awkwardness had come from or when it had begun; nothing had been said, but there was a distance now which she knew would be difficult to cross.

Halfway there, he stopped the coach and got out, finishing the journey on horseback.

She had forgotten the painting of her predecessor which still leaned against the wall in her bedchamber. It was too late to have it taken away; he had got there first and she entered the chamber to see him staring down at it, as though it were some strange animal which had crept into the house.

"Well," he said. "You will want to ask me about her, no doubt."

"Yes," she replied. "She was your wife before me. I do not understand why you told me nothing about her, not even that she ever existed."

He turned and looked at her earnestly, as though wondering whether to answer.

"Because I would rather not have to think about her," he replied quietly.

Her heart went out to him. Her guess had been right; he had put her portrait away in the attic because he did not want to be reminded of her.

"Because you loved her so much?"

He frowned, then a little mocking grin appeared on his lips.

"No, my love, because I could not stand the sight of her." He lay down on the bed and stared up at the ceiling, then held out his hand to her and pulled her down with him. "I was not immune to the schemes of my parents. I was young, the marriage had been arranged since we were children. I don't think I had met her more than once, but my father assured me she was a good match. I expect her father told her the same thing."

She put her hand on his chest to comfort him and he gripped it tightly.

"You asked me why I applied to you for your hand and not your father," he went on. "She was the reason. All I wanted was a companion, hopefully a son, but she was terrified of me. If I spoke to her she jumped. Sometimes I would catch sight of her quickly hiding when she saw me coming. There was no talking to her, no finding out what troubled her. I did try, but she refused to speak to me, just sat rigid as though I might do her some harm."

He sounded angry as he spoke and she felt his body tensing, wished she had never ventured into the attics.

"I could not make love to her; she spent the time weeping. I felt rejected, I admit it. It was my first time, or should have been and I thought perhaps it would always be like that."

"Should have been?" She asked hesitantly.

"Yes. It never happened; the marriage was never consummated. She was so frightened I thought she might die of shock and that made me feel inadequate. Another man might have forced her, but I could not do that." He paused, his mouth turned down in a grimace. "Instead I went and found myself a woman for hire. She was but the first of many, until I realised it was not my fault."

"That is why you asked if I knew…"

"Yes. And I swore if I ever had the chance to marry again, it would be to a woman who wanted me. Rosemary was a child; she should never have married anyone."

So this was the reason he had not tried to bed her on their wedding night, that he could not make love to a woman who was crying.

"Anthony said she died of plague."

"She did and it was my fault. I could not stand to have her near me any longer, so I sent her to London to live with my aunt and uncle. Anthony was coming here to learn how a nobleman should live; it seemed a fair exchange. But plague struck and they all died."

"Do you feel guilty about that? Is that why you buried her picture beneath a pile of landscapes?"

He looked puzzled as though he had never considered the matter before.

"No, sweetheart. I am sorry to disappoint you, but I have never felt guilty. What I felt was that the hand of God played a part in her going there at that time. I felt relieved and I thank Him every day for freeing me from such a burden."

She sat up and looked down at him, shocked and not really sure whether this was some new scheme to drive her away. That was certainly what he had seemed to be doing since she joined him in London.

"Are you shocked?" He asked. "Well don't be. You want the truth, do you not?"

"I pity her," she said softly.

"So did I. That was one of the reasons I could not bear to be near her. How can you have respect for someone whom you pity?"

They lay quietly for a long time while she wondered what to say to him. There seemed to be nothing.

"So you will return to London?" She asked at last. He nodded. "When will I see you again?"

"I shall be back from time to time. Right now, Mary is still deciding how best to bring England back to the church. She is not keen on taking things slowly, as her advisors would have her do. But she knows that she must be strong and execute Jane Grey and Guildford Dudley, although she is reluctant. There will be plots to put them back on the throne. The Duke's fate is already sealed."

"But Jane Grey is little more than a child. She can have had no real say in what went on."

"That is true." He turned his head to look down at her. "I am not concerned with her fate, but I am concerned with yours. I want you to stay here, at Summerville, no matter what the Queen might want. I do not want to risk your safety by having you at court." He kissed the top of her head affectionately, as though she were a sister instead of a wife. "I have enemies, Bethany, and they are always looking for an opportunity to bring me down. It is the way when someone is in favour with the monarch. You cannot pretend; I saw it the first time I met you and I saw it when you met the Queen. God knows, it was one of the things which attracted me to you in the first place. Having you there will destroy me, and ultimately destroy you, too."

Did he mean to protect her, she wondered? Or only to protect himself?

"The Queen has requested that you serve her as a lady in waiting," he said suddenly. "I cannot allow that."

Her heart sank even deeper in the depression she had been feeling. She could not be that close to Mary and he knew it, but would he ever forgive her for that?

"What will you tell her?" She asked.

"For now, I shall tell her you are ill. But that cannot suffice indefinitely."

She looked up at him, at the worried frown he wore, then she caressed his cheek.

"She will not expect me at Court if you tell her I am with child," she said carefully, watching for his reaction. She had not wanted to tell him under these circumstances, but it seemed the only thing she could do to forestall his resentment. His eyes searched hers, as though looking for some sign of deception.

"Are you? Really?"

"I think so. I wanted to be sure before I told you. I did not want to disappoint you."

She expected him to kiss her, to show his joy at this news, but instead he got up from the bed and turned to look down at her suspiciously.

"I shall be back as soon as I can," he murmured thoughtfully.

Her heart hurt with those words, that he was going anyway. She had hoped her news might make him stay with her, if only for a few days. She was not sure she would be able to bear it, but she refused to show him how weak and helpless she felt. He had despised Rosemary because she aroused pity in him; she would not have the same felt for her.

But that closeness between them had vanished and she could not let him go without at least trying to recover it.

"Will you do something for me before you go?"

"Of course. Anything."

"Will you make love to me? Give me something to live on until I see you again."

He sat down beside her on the bed, then took her into his arms.

"Is it quite safe?" He asked.

She nodded, not really sure whether it was or not. She had heard it was a sure way to bring on a miscarriage, but she believed that to be a rumour started by the church, who preached that intimacy in marriage was there for the procreation of children and nothing else.

He started to unfasten her clothing, while his lips travelled down her neck and over her breasts. Then he held her face between his hands and forced her to look up at him. He sighed wistfully.

"Why did you have to fall in love with me?" He whispered. "I did not want that. Now I fear you will be badly hurt and that was not my plan, not at all."

"I will not be hurt if you stay with me, Richard. If you give me a chance to make you love me back."

He gently stroked her cheek with his thumb and gave her a warm smile. Then he shook his head slowly; he did not want her to know he already did love her, did not want to return to London without her. She would be far better off not knowing

CHAPTER FIVE

It was Christmas before she saw him again and by that time she was getting big with child and felt very unattractive. She had received only a few letters from him but none had spoken of his business in London. There was little to say and it was never wise to put one's thoughts into writing, lest they fall into the wrong hands.

She had not been able to ride out in search of her sister, but she had sent servants looking for her and carrying funds in case she should need them. They had been told she had moved on, that no word of her was now known. They had also been told that she had given birth to a son whom she had naturally taken with her.

There was but one reason Julia would run away to fend for herself with a baby, and that reason was clear. The child did not belong to her husband and judging by the display Bethany had witnessed in Sir Geoffrey's house he most probably knew it. But although she tried to deny it to herself, it was clear to her just whose child it was. It was certainly possible. There had been an unseemly familiarity between the two and it would certainly explain her outrage at the marriage. She pushed the treacherous thought away, hoping she was wrong, but there was no one else. She would not think of it now, not when she was about to see Richard for the first time in months.

She was waiting outside when he rode up on his beautiful black horse and swung himself out of the saddle. A groom came swiftly to take the reins and lead the animal away, while Richard caught Bethany in his arms and held her close.

Anthony was behind her, waiting to greet his cousin with enthusiasm.

"I have missed you," he declared, shaking Richard's hand vigorously. "I hope I have not made too much of a mess of things."

"I am sure you have not." He put his arm around his wife and they all walked inside together. "You are cold," he said. "You should not have been waiting outside in that flimsy gown."

He ordered wine and bread and they sat around a roaring fire, Richard next to her on the settle. He put his hand on her swollen stomach and felt the child kick, then smiled with satisfaction.

"All is well?" He asked.

"I hope so. There have been no problems."

He nodded, then turned to Anthony.

"I will hear whether you have left me penniless when I have rested," he told him with a laugh. "For now, I need to be alone with my wife."

Her heart leapt at his words. She wanted desperately to be alone with him, too, but she doubted he had the same thing in mind, not considering her condition. She was soon to discover his intentions could not be farther from hers.

Anthony cheerfully went away while Richard turned and kissed her, then pulled her head down onto his shoulder. She thought he might tell her he had missed her but she was wrong. He had something to say which he did not want Anthony or anyone else to hear.

"We have guests coming for the festive period," he began at once. "There are some things I need you to know before they come so you will not behave in an unseemly manner should you find out from them."

She looked up at him, hurt at this slight and that hurt clearly showed in her eyes.

"Why have you invited guests when you know I cannot be seen?"

His dark eyes swept over her stomach again and he took her hand.

"I had little choice. These are important people and the Queen asked me to have them here; she seems to think they should get to know me better."

He suspected there was another reason, but Bethany had no need to know of it.

"The Queen is becoming zealous in her efforts to wipe out heresy," he told her. "You may have heard that more people have been put to death in the last weeks."

"I have," she replied. "It is not something I want to think about."

"So you do not believe their deaths are deserved? You do not believe that by suffering the flames here on earth, they will be spared them in purgatory?"

"Of course not. Do you?"

He pushed her away then.

"I knew you would never be able to follow me," he said harshly. "I was attracted to you because you were so open and honest, because you could not pretend. And here I thought I could make you into something you are not." He got to his feet, shaking his head. "It is my fault. It is unlikely you will be required to voice an opinion before our guests, but if you are, have a care what you say."

"But Richard! You do not believe that, do you?"

"I wanted to see what your reaction would be, as this is the sort of talk that will be heard from our guests. Your condition will be a good enough reason for your absence."

Then he bowed to her and disappeared upstairs, leaving her to wonder how her future would turn out, or indeed if she even had a future.

The house was full of high born Catholic lords and ladies in the days leading up to and after Christmas and she waited in vain for Richard to join her in her bedchamber. She had so looked forward to spending a quiet Christmas together, but now all she could do was have her meals sent to her chamber and listen to the chatter coming from the great hall, the minstrels and the music.

She was upset that he had invited all these people, knowing that by custom she could not show herself. Not once was she alone with him, not once did she have an opportunity to talk to him and she felt he had arranged things that way. Just like when she met him in London, he seemed to be trying to push her away, trying to distance himself from her and damage the love he knew she felt for him.

There was no longer any need to follow the underground passage to the church, so the guests donned their outdoor clothing and walked across the field to the woods. She had hoped that, since she could not be seen for the festivities, she would not be expected to attend mass either, but her hope was in vain. Richard ordered the carriage for her, deeming it too much walking, and she was heavily cloaked to conceal her figure. It seemed that even a woman heavily pregnant was not to be excused the midnight mass on Christmas Eve.

The masses she had so far knelt through had been tedious and each one had made her feel farther and farther away from God, but this mass was the worst of all. She could no longer kneel, she was too heavy, but she stood for hours for the service, the most important one, and when it was over, she half expected the gates of hell to be awaiting her on the other side of the doors.

Although she had been given a chair halfway through, she was still exhausted and had difficulty getting to her feet. She looked about for a servant to help her, assuming her husband to be too busy with his guests to notice. But Richard was at her side at once, gripping her around the waist and helping her up. She felt the first sharp pain in that church and was sure she was about to be punished at last for her betrayal.

"Quickly!" He called to whoever wanted to hear. "Her Ladyship is ill. Bring the carriage up to the door at once."

Then he lifted her into his arms and carried her outside, where he climbed into the carriage beside her, calling to his servants to send for a physician. It was much too early for the child to be born.

He sat beside the bed holding his wife's hand while they waited for the physician to arrive and by the time he did, the pain had stopped.

"The strain of the mass, My Lady," the physician said confidently. "All that standing is too much for a woman of your delicate condition. You should rest, stay in bed until the time for your confinement."

"That is months away!"

"No matter," Richard said. "You must not risk your safety again, nor that of the child."

He felt sure this early danger sign was his fault. He had been unkind to her when he arrived, partly because he was more afraid than ever now to get too close, but also because the Queen was still insisting his wife serve her once she had recovered from the birth. He did not want to admit that he harboured some resentment about her failure to behave as she had promised him. It was not her fault yet he knew his attitude to her had caused her pain, and now this risk to their child was the result.

When the physician had gone and he leaned over the bed to kiss her goodnight, she clasped his hand and held it against her lips. He sat on the bed beside her.

"Stay with me," she said. "I have not seen you for months and here you bring all these strangers into our home and do not even spend one night with me. Is that really too much to ask?"

Tears brimmed in her eyes and she tried desperately to keep the misery out of her voice, but she could not help it. She was showing him weakness she felt he would not approve of, she was afraid such weakness would arouse his pity, but soon he would return to London and she would not see him again for weeks. All she wanted was one night alone with him.

"Bethany," he said soothingly. "Forgive me, please. You are heavy with child."

"And repulsive to you?"

"Of course not. But it is not customary for a man to spend time in his wife's bed when she is so close to the birth."

Ah, so this was another custom of the nobility she had failed to observe.

"I want nothing from you," she said. "Only your arms around me, only your comfort. But if that is beneath your noble dignity, I quite understand. You had best go before I disgrace you further."

The catch in her voice almost brought him to tears. Why had he not realised she would think him uncaring?

"I honestly thought you would not want me here at this time," he said.

He swung his legs up to lie beside her and gathered her into his arms, his lips came down on hers and he kissed her before pulling her head onto his chest where she listened to the rapid pulsing of his heart as she drifted into sleep.

He returned to London a few days later, only waiting to be sure she was fully recovered. She did rest, but she only stayed in bed long enough to feel the child move once more. Perhaps the physician had been right; perhaps it had been the strain of standing for too long.

Or perhaps God was telling her it was not to be. She would not know until the birth. She would shut herself away with her women before that, she would disappear into her confinement chamber where no man was allowed.

The first pains came at the beginning of March when the wind whipped around the house but the dark chamber was airless. The midwife came and ran her rough old hands over Bethany's stomach, squeezing to test if the baby was in the birth position.

"Lord Summerville?" She asked quietly. "Has he been sent for?"

"I believe so, My Lady," she replied. "Mr Anthony sent a messenger this morning. He should have arrived in London by now." She carried on examining her patient, shaking her head as she did so. Bethany got the impression she did not approve of sending for a father when a baby was about to be born.

"Is it all well?" She asked her.

"It is, My Lady. You will have an easy birth, I think, God willing." Then she produced a dish of jet and poured some water into it. "Drink this, My Lady. It will ease the pain."

Bethany had heard of such things as jet dishes to ease the pain of childbirth, but she did not know they were still used. She was even more surprised, and fearful, to see what the woman did next.

She took the dish and put it aside, while from her bag she produced a scroll. It was a prayer scroll of St Margaret, the patron saint of women in labour. She placed it over Bethany's stomach to ease the pain of childbirth. This was a catholic custom, one which had been abandoned and was now frowned upon, or at least it had been during King Edward's reign.

She felt it was papist superstition, even felt it might harm her baby, and she longed to pull it off and throw it away, but of course she could not refuse. Perhaps it could do no harm; after all, women had used this same protection for centuries and harm had not befallen all of them. But God was already angry with her and she was afraid.

Where was Richard? This was what he had been waiting for, this is what he had married her for, so why was he not here? She wanted him, she needed him. He knew when the child was likely to be born, so why had he not come already?

Many women died in childbirth. It was a dangerous time, especially for a first child, and she wanted him to sit by her side and feel some of the fear that was hers, but even if he had arrived, he would not be allowed inside the birthing chamber. That was a place for females only. But she recalled his abrupt dismissal of the women on their wedding night, recalled the affront of the older one when he ignored the custom of centuries. She was sure that if he wanted to come in, no midwife would keep him out.

The birth was easy compared to some of the horror stories she had heard throughout her life. It was not so many hours before her daughter was born and afterwards she slept, exhausted.

She awoke to see Richard bending over the wooden crib which was placed beside the bed, the tiny hand wrapped around his finger, and recalled why he had married her. He had wanted an heir, someone who could take over when he was gone, someone who would inherit the title. He must be so disappointed! That thought distressed her terribly, despite his recent scathing remarks.

"I am sorry, My Lord," she whispered.

She felt distanced from him now and did not feel comfortable in using his first name. He turned to face her, then came and sat on the bed taking her hand.

"For what?"

"For the baby being a girl."

"Do you think I mind that?" He said with a gentle smile. "I was concerned that you may not conceive at all, I will confess, but you have proved yourself capable of producing a healthy child." He brought her fingers to his lips and kissed them. "A boy next time, perhaps. If God is willing."

Her immediate thought was to ask why God should want to help either of them, but she knew it would be a dangerous thing to say. That was why she could no longer use his Christian name. He had changed since living at court, since being close to the Queen and she feared him now, feared what he would do should she speak her thoughts.

But his mention of a boy next time had cheered her. At least he intended to return, if only for that.

He climbed up beside her, rested his head on the headboard and sat on the bed beside her, put his arm around her, and took from his purse a small, velvet pouch, which he gave to her. She tipped the contents into her hand and found herself gazing at a sparkling, diamond ring.

"A gift for the mother of my child," he said.

He took it from her hand and slipped it onto her finger.

"Thank you," she murmured. "It is beautiful."

"I hope it fits. I had it made specially."

She felt his fingers on her chin, tilting her face up and his lips came down and kissed her, that special kiss which only he could give, and for the first time in months she felt that perhaps he did love her after all.

"I must return to London tomorrow," he said after a moment. "The Queen is asking for her advisors to be ready for her impending marriage. I would like to have a say in proceedings, for all our sakes."

"What does that mean?"

He seemed about to tell her, then he changed his mind and just shook his head slowly.

"It is better that you not know," he said. "I want you to promise that you will take care of yourself, and of the little one. Have you arranged for a wet nurse?"

It was not something she had considered and she realised someone should have been found long before this. She supposed it was not the accepted thing for a countess to breastfeed her child herself. Once again, she found herself wondering how best to reply, and this was not a situation she enjoyed.

"I do not want one, My Lord," she replied.

"Good."

"You approve? I am surprised."

"Why? It is not natural to allow another woman so much intimacy with one's child. You are her mother, after all. I do not approve of your sudden reversion to my title, though. What is that all about?"

"It seemed you were angry with me the last time you were here."

He leaned across and kissed her gently.

"I was and I was wrong to be angry. Will you forgive me?"

She only nodded then decided to change the subject.

"What name would you like for your daughter, Richard?" The name stuck in her throat a little, but he seemed not to notice. "I would like Elizabeth, after my mother."

"No," he said at once. "The Queen would take that as the greatest insult."

Of course she would; why had she not thought of that? Her sister was her greatest rival and enemy.

"I do not want her called Mary," she said quickly, then wondered if she had made him angry, but his expression remained unchanged.

"What do you want to call her? Anything, but not Elizabeth and not Jane."

"Alicia," She said suddenly. "It was my grandmother's name. How would that be?"

"That would be perfect," he replied with a smile. "Then we will arrange the baptism for this afternoon, before I return to London."

The baptism. Another long, gruelling and treacherous Catholic ceremony. Another chance for her to be struck down by an angry God. Since she was confined to bed, she was not required to attend, but that did not stop her from feeling even farther away from God.

She must have been mad to think she could accept all this, but it was not going to be real, was it? Jane Grey was going to be Queen, the country was going to remain Protestant. But she knew nothing then about the church in the woods, nor about the priest who was hidden away in the little cottage beside it.

She was sure there was no way back to God for her; she had even given her only child into the arms of the idolaters.

***

Although there were two full time nurses for the baby, she was glad she had refused a wet nurse. She had fallen in love with this tiny creature and she fascinated Bethany. She did not much care whether it was seemly for a woman in her position to want to spend every waking moment with her child. She kept her occupied and her mind on something other than what Richard might be doing at court.

Every little development was fascinating, from her first smile to her first attempt at sitting up. It was early summer and with a little help from some pillows she sat up in the crib and laughed at her mother. What a wonderful gift God had given her, even though she did not deserve it. That thought made her realise how easily He could take it away, that perhaps He was building up for a greater punishment.

She had regular letters from Richard, but they contained nothing but minor news of what was happening in London. Mary had been busy rounding up Protestants, trying to force them to recant their heresies, and condemning them to a horrible death if they refused. She was not as popular now as she had been on her accession to the throne, that was for certain, but she was strong willed and would do things her own way, no matter what her advisors had to say about it.

It was a pity. She was the first Queen of England in her own right and she had the opportunity to show the world once and for all that a woman could rule. Instead she was making it impossible for anyone to believe that. The Empress Matilda, in the twelfth century, should have been Queen but the people had chosen her cousin, Stephen, simply because she was a woman. She was a strong woman, though, stronger than Mary. She had started a war to regain her throne and peace only reigned when Stephen agreed to make her son his heir.

Mary's only concern was to turn England back to the Church of Rome, no matter what destruction she left in her wake. Priests who had been allowed to marry under the rule of King Edward were ordered to abandon their wives or they would be thrown in the street with no pension and would starve.

The former Archbishop Cranmer was one of those priests, and he declared he had left his wife, although whether he really had nobody knew for sure. Bethany was quite disappointed, as he had been a Protestant figure they all respected. He had been replaced as Archbishop and arrested for heresy, despite having saved

Mary's life once when he had pleaded with King Henry on her behalf. She did not care that Cranmer had been like a kind uncle during her childhood; he was a heretic, and that was the only thing that counted.

Alicia was four months old now, and it was a fine day. Summer had been warm that year and the nurse had taken the baby for a walk around the grounds to get some fresh air. Whilst Bethany normally went with them, as fate would have it, this day she was sitting under a tree reading her latest letter from her mother.

When her father found out just how important his son-in-law was at the court of Queen Mary, he had been furious and had chosen to disown both his daughters. Julia had committed the ultimate sin by leaving her husband, whom it was her duty to love, even if he had no love or even respect for her, while Bethany had become a Catholic and supported her husband. Of course she would have been just as outcast had she not supported her husband, so either way he would have turned against her. But her mother secretly wrote to tell her what was happening. On this occasion she told her that she and her father were selling all they could and fleeing to France, where the Huguenots were helping the English Protestants to avoid the wrath of the new Queen of England.

Bethany heard the sound of hoofs approaching the house, but assumed it was probably someone wanting Anthony, who was the head of the house now. She thought a lot about his feelings in all this and wondered just how much it was safe to tell him. Certainly her mother's letter would be consigned to the flames as soon as she could sneak into the kitchens with it. She dare not ask for a fire to be lit when the weather was still so warm; it would only arouse suspicion. If there was one thing she had learned about the loyal Catholics is that they were always suspicious of anything out of the ordinary, always looking for signs of heresy.

The secret evacuation of Protestants to France was a new thing and not one that was widely known. The longer it was kept secret the better.

When she heard the footsteps crunching in the grass she finally looked up to see Richard smiling down at her. The safety of her mother's letter flew from her mind at the sight of him and her heart skipped. He reached down, took her hand and pulled her to her feet, then took her face gently in his hands and kissed her, the long, passionate kiss she had half forgotten. She put her arms around his waist and held on to him as tightly as she could, wanting to squeeze him into her, wanting to meld her body with his.

"Why did you not write?" She asked. "I did not expect you. I have nothing prepared."

"I need nothing, except to see you and my little girl," he replied with a smile, then he held her against him. Could it be that he had really missed her?

"The nurse has taken Alicia," she said quickly. "I will send someone after them at once."

"No need. There is plenty of time. I shall be staying for a night or two."

The self control she had built around her emotions disintegrated like so much fog when the sun comes out. He was staying? He caught her hand and walked with her back toward the house; she did not see him glance back at the discarded letter beneath the oak tree.

***

Anthony waited at the door of the house, a huge welcoming smile on his freckled face. They had estate business to discuss and Bethany was happy to leave them alone for the time being. She went upstairs, wondering how she would control herself enough to seem distant when that was the last thing she felt, but that seemed to be what he wanted. Mary was slowly building a wall between them, another brick built each time she saw him, and soon it would be too high to see over, much less tear down.

He would still be wanting an heir. He had said so after she gave birth to Alicia. *A boy next time,* that was what he had said. Perhaps that is what had brought him home so unexpectedly.

Bethany lie on her bed and stared at the ceiling, her memory showing her his gentle lovemaking, his fingers brushing her skin, his strength inside her and that little thrill of anticipation ran through her again. She wanted him so much, she thought she might die of it.

It was a couple of hours later she remembered her letter and began to search her gown for it, then she suddenly realised she had dropped it on the ground outside. She ran down the staircase and out into the grounds, back to the oak tree where she had been reading when Richard interrupted her. There was no wind, it should still be there. But it was gone.

She searched thoroughly, she asked the servants if they had been outside but none of them had and when Alicia's nurse returned with the baby, she questioned her as well. She denied having been that way before, but given the contents of the letter and given that every single person on this property was fiercely loyal to Richard and Queen Mary, she had no idea who to trust.

She took the child from the nurse and went inside to present her to her father.

Watching him with the baby, she felt sad that she could not recall any such intimacy between her father and any of his children. Richard played with the little girl, even hiding behind chairs to pop his head out and make her laugh. The interaction warmed her heart and made her wish they were just a quiet working family who could spend time together, instead of him being so important at court.

It was late when he finally joined her. She had been lying awake, wishing he would come and wondering why he did not, wondering why he was not as hungry for her as she was for him. She also wondered desperately who had found her mother's letter. There had been nobody about except the two of them, but anything could have happened while she rested on her bed. It could even be that one of the dogs had come along and taken it.

"Still awake?" He asked as he entered the chamber. "I have kept you waiting. Forgive me. The child is thriving, is she not? The nurse tells me she is a fine, healthy baby."

"She is wonderful," she replied.

He finished undressing then climbed into the bed beside her.

"She needs a brother," he said quietly as he began to run his hands over her body, sending a wave of desire throbbing through her being. "I have missed you."

He bent his dark head to her breast and took it into his mouth. It had been so long since she felt his arms around her, since she felt him inside her, the pleasure was almost painful. But she had been right; he had come to try for another child, a boy this time, and nothing more.

They lay together in silence, her head resting on his bare chest.

"I wish you could stay," she murmured quietly. "I miss you so much when you are away."

"I cannot," he replied. "That is what I came to tell you. The Queen is planning to marry next month and there will be much to organise."

Her heart sank. She could no longer stay away on the excuse of being with child. Was it possible she was to be dragged into the Queen's presence for the wedding? When she realised that was not his plan, she did not know whether to be disappointed or joyous.

"I told you I do not want you at court," he said. "That has not changed. You must stay here at Summerville; do not even think of coming to London, not even to visit. Do I have your word?"

His voice sounded urgent. Willingly she nodded her agreement; she had no desire to go to London again, but she thought demanding her word on the matter a little extreme.

"Her choice of husband will not be popular," he went on. "It is possible there will be uprisings, many factions wanting to replace her with Elizabeth. I shall have to defend her; I may not return."

She sat up and looked at him, terrified by his words and feeling used once more. He had been anxious for an early marriage date in case he was killed defending this little woman with the mad staring eyes. Now he had come only to try for an heir before he laid down his life for her once more.

She had never felt so hurt, but she tried her best to hide it. It was what he had married for, was it not? It was what she had agreed to and he had promised nothing more. Was it his fault that she revelled in his presence? Was it his fault that she adored the very ground beneath his feet?

"Who is she going to marry?" She murmured quietly, not really caring.

"Prince Philip of Spain."

"No!" She cried. "She cannot marry him. He will bring the inquisition here."

"It is settled, and nothing I can do about it. He wants to be crowned King, though, and I don't think she is so infatuated as to allow that. But she is hoping for an heir." He paused and lay his palm on her stomach. "As am I."

"She is too old to bear a child," she said without thinking. It was one of those times when she wished she could grab back the words, but his expression did not change.

"You may be right, but anything is possible. She believes that despite her age, God will be on her side and grant her a healthy son. After all, the mother of John the Baptist was well past child-bearing age." He paused and pulled her back down beside him. "I am more concerned with what she will do if she does not produce a son."

She was startled to hear him talking like this. He always kept his opinions about the Queen to himself.

"What do you mean?"

"No matter," he said holding her close to him. "I am only telling you that this is the last time you will see me for a very long time. And you may not hear from me either."

He reached across to where he had left his doublet on the end of the bed and pulled out a familiar piece of paper. It was the missing letter. Once more she feared what he would do; it was as if she had never really known him at all. But she had not. She knew nothing about him when they married, nothing except he was very wealthy and a Catholic. He held the letter out to her and she took it, her fingers trembling.

"Burn it," he said. "It is treason. You must have more care."

***

He stayed one more night. This time he took her hand and led her to her bedchamber after supper, dismissed the servants and undressed her himself as he had in the early days, and she felt sure he was not doing this only for a son. She had missed this closeness, this love and as she lie in his arms and kissed his nipple, she wished

Queen Mary dead so that every night could be like this one.

The next day he left her wondering why he had not used the letter to uncover a Protestant secret of the greatest magnitude. Such information would raise him even higher in the eyes of the Queen, yet he had returned the letter to his wife to destroy. Of course, he did not need it to warn of the Protestants' escape plans; there were no specific details in it, as her mother would not have been privy to them. He had told her to burn the letter in order to protect her family, and by association to protect his wife. But she was still unsure he was really trying to protect her and not himself. Mary would not be pleased to know his wife had Protestant parents, would she?

She gradually came to understand that her husband was a very important advisor to the Queen and as such she wondered why Mary did not insist that his wife attend her. Surely he must have run out of excuses to explain her absence, especially as she had requested her as a lady in waiting? She did not want to ask; she was just happy for it to be this way.

The marriage between Queen Mary and Prince Philip took place on the 25th July 1554 and in October of that same year it was announced that the Queen was with child. The news terrified Bethany, but her feelings on the subject had to be kept hidden as the rest of the household were overjoyed. Father O'Neil held a special mass to pray for Her Majesty and the safe deliverance of a healthy son, which Her Ladyship had to attend or arouse suspicion.

Alicia was growing fast and was now no longer dependant on breast milk. She needed more substantial food.

Richard's words were beginning to penetrate as she heard nothing from him, nothing at all. His letters had ceased altogether, although Anthony still received instructions about the estate. Her heart leapt whenever she saw his handwriting or his seal, but there was never anything for her. Why not? And why had she not asked him at the time why he could not write to his wife? Because she had not really been listening, that was why. She was too happy to have him back in her bed to pay attention to a warning which seemed in the far distant future.

At the back of Bethany's mind there had always been Julia, worrying away at her while she tried to get on with being a mother. With Richard away and unlikely to return any time soon, she decided it was time she found her. She wanted only to assure herself that Julia was safe, that she had enough funds to live comfortably. She had not been able to leave Alicia before, since she needed her mother, but she admitted to herself that she had been putting it off since she learned her sister had a son.

Anthony had once more sent Richard's contact out looking for her, and had found another place where she might be. This was a farm some five miles away, so she took two male servants and set out early one morning.

"I am not happy about this," Anthony said. "Richard would not want you to go off on your own to an unknown place. How do you know it is safe?"

"I do not. Richard would not try to stop me, so what gives you the right?"

"I am not trying to stop you, Bethany. Richard would insist on going with you though, and so will I."

"No," She said putting her hand on his chest to stop him following. "I need you to oversee the nurses, to be sure my daughter is safe."

"Are you saying you do not trust them?"

"I do, but they are after all only employed. You are her cousin; you really care for her. I shall not be easy leaving her otherwise."

He finally agreed, but reluctantly and only because the place was so close.

The roads were quiet enough and there was a sharp pinch of winter in the air, despite the sunshine. It was drawing toward Christmas and Bethany was glad she saw no horrors on her journey. Sometimes there were women with babies begging on the road and although she always found them something, they had the effect of making her feel guilty for having so much. She had thought she was so unfortunate before she met Richard, yet here were people who did not know if they or their children would eat that day.

When they finally arrived at the farm, she saw there were a few scattered cottages not far from the entrance and surrounded by fields. In the distance was a large manor house which looked deserted but there were a few horses grazing in the paddock and some saddles over the rails outside the cottages.

They drew rein before the first of them and a young man came out, frowning suspiciously, to enquire as to their business.

He was a good looking man, about thirty years old, with reddish blonde hair and beard but his expression was almost savage. He stood with his arms folded before the doorway, as though guarding it. She wondered not who he was, but why he should be so hostile to strangers.

"Sir," she said. "I am looking for my sister. Her name is Julia, Lady Winterton. She has blonde hair and..."

"I know Lady Winterton," he interrupted.

"You do? You know where I can find her?"

"That depends. She came here to escape her kin. If you are truly her sister, she may not wish to see you."

Bethany was astonished that this hostile stranger would tell her that her own sister might be hiding from her. He had made her angry, which in turn made her less fearful.

"Who are you, Sir," she demanded, "to suggest my sister may not wish to see me?"

She felt this man was controlling Julia's actions. She was not prepared to put up with that, but she stayed mounted just the same. She was definitely safer on horseback.

"It is all right, Charles," a familiar voice came from the cottage behind him. There was a movement in the doorway of the cottage and Julia appeared, wearing the clothes of a peasant but otherwise unchanged. She gazed at her. "Bethany, why have you come? And does His Lordship know you are here?"

Bethany dismounted and moved toward her, intending to take her in her arms, but she stepped away deliberately, with a look of distaste on her face. So nothing had changed. She had disowned her sister and despite her assumption that she had not meant it, it seems she was wrong.

"I have come to find you," Bethany replied. "Why did you run off without a word? I could have helped you, given you money."

"It was for the best," she replied quietly. "I had some valuable jewels to sell; I survived." Then she turned to the man she had called Charles. "Would you take my sister's servants and give them refreshments."

"Are you quite sure she can be trusted?" He replied. "Knowing to whom she is wed, I would not trust her."

"She is my sister, Charles. She will not betray us."

Bethany had no idea what they were talking about and she had not come all this way to cause trouble, so she followed Julia without a word to him. She watched her two servants go with him toward the manor house, still wondering why he was so hostile and what he had meant by 'knowing to whom she is wed'.

Inside, the little cottage was cosy but the air was chill. There were no luxuries, no fine furnishings, just the basic needs of everyday living. There was a cauldron hanging over the fire and a further room in which she could just make out the corner of a large bed.

Julia handed her a tankard of ale just as a small boy appeared at the door to the bedchamber. He was about two years old and his resemblance to one of the miniatures at Summerville Hall was so great, it could have been the same child. Bethany's suspicions were confirmed; she knew at once why she had run away.

"This is Richard's son?" She asked softly.

"Can you see now why I did not want you to marry him?" Julia demanded. "He would have helped me, he would have found me a place. I could have been happy enough as yet another of his mistresses. But it was all too late once you accepted him; I could not tell him then."

"You mean he does not know? He does not know he has a son?"

"No, and you must promise not to tell him."

Bethany simply stared at her for a few minutes, imagining a scenario in which she would tell her husband he had a healthy son by another woman. The idea made her shudder.

"Why would I do that? You have his son and I do not, so why would I want him to know that? I just wanted to be sure you were safe."

"I am with Charles now," she said softly.

"And does he know? Does he know your child is not your husband's?"

"No, he does not. He believes I left my husband because he ill treated me and that is no lie. He does not know the truth about Simon." She paused and closed her eyes for a few seconds. "If he had any idea who Simon's father was, I am not certain of what he would do."

"Just what was he talking about before? What is there to betray? He wasn't only talking about you, was he?"

"It is not important," she replied. "Just believe that I love Charles, he has taken me and my son and will care for us as best he can. I will say no more. You cannot expect either one of us to trust the wife of the most feared and hated man in England."

Bethany stepped back, totally shattered by her words.

"Richard?" She whispered. "Do you mean Richard?"

"Of course. He is at the right hand of the fanatic. He will be helping her devise ways to trap loyal Protestants and send them to the stake. That is what he does, Bethany. Are you saying you did not know?"

She was shaking her head slowly, utterly bewildered by her sister's words.

"You are wrong," she insisted. "He would never do such a thing. He is trying to make her curb her enthusiasm, trying to make her convert the Protestants peacefully."

"I am glad to hear you call us Protestants and not heretics at least. It shows he has not managed to corrupt you completely."

"He has not corrupted me at all."

"You knew he was Catholic when you married him. You were prepared to turn for his wealth."

Bethany took a deep breath and swallowed.

"I cannot deny it. Just as you knew what he was when you let him take you to his bed."

"It was one afternoon of comfort, Bethany, that is all," she answered with a weary sigh. "I did not promise to join the papists and idolaters in exchange for his wealth. Now you know how Judas Iscariot must have felt when he realised what he had done for his thirty pieces of silver."

Tears sprang to Bethany's eyes at her words. She could not believe she was hearing them from her and she turned and fled from the cottage. Julia had likened her to the man who sent the Saviour to the cross? She climbed onto her horse and called her servants to follow. She had to get away. All those months worrying about her, and this was all the thanks she got for seeking her out, for ensuring her safety. Harsh words and a bastard child who should have been hers!

CHAPTER SIX

Bethany could barely see through her tears as she rode home and was relieved to be able to give her horse to a groom and hurry back inside the house. Julia's words had repeated over and over on the journey, both her judgment of Bethany and of her husband. She had to know what she meant, she had to know if it was true.

Inside she went straight to Anthony.

"Is it true?" She demanded. "Is Richard the most hated man in England?"

"What on earth are you talking about?" He said as he rose to his feet to come and stand before her.

"I was told that is what he is to Protestants. I was told they fear him more than any other, that his sole objective is to find them and send them to their deaths." She paused and looked up at him for a reaction, anything that might tell her it was a lie. He was never good at concealing his feelings. "Is it true?"

He shook his head slowly, a sign that he was about to evade the question.

"You need to ask Richard these things, Bethany. It is not my place to answer your questions."

"Is that all you ever say?" She demanded harshly. "I will have to ask Richard? Do you not have a mind of your own?"

He made no reply, merely turned back to what he had been doing.

"Very well," she said at last. "I shall have to find out for myself. I shall have to go to London and see how the land lies there."

He spun around, moving faster than she had ever seen him move before as he grabbed her wrist.

"No!" He shouted. "You must not."

She looked down at his grip on her wrist until he released her.

"Who are you to tell me I must not? Are you then my gaoler, after all?"

"Please, Bethany, do not force me to betray my promises. Stay here, where it is safe. It is what Richard wanted."

"I know what he wanted, but I need to know the truth. Can you not see that?"

It was a long time before he answered. It was not hard to guess that he had promised Richard to keep his wife here, and she was asking him to break that promise, but she could never have guessed just how deep that promise went. She could not guess at the real reason she was to stay at Summerville, but he knew he had to tell her. It was the only way to make her stay.

"You cannot simply announce yourself at court," he insisted.

"Why not? My husband has a position and apartments there, so why should I not visit him? How can that possibly be construed as suspicious?"

She watched him as he made up his mind what he should do. He was growing into a fine man, but was still afraid to act without approval, lest he make a mistake. He had promised his cousin he would keep her away from court, that was obvious, and now he was wondering if it was worth breaking that promise.

"If you go to court," he said slowly, having made up his mind, "you might well be the cause of his death. Is that what you want?"

She laughed then. Did he have to be so dramatic?

"How you exaggerate, Anthony. Am I supposed to abandon my plan because you have come up with the worst scenario you can think of? How would my going to court cause Richard's death, pray?"

The idea seemed so ridiculous she could barely keep a straight face. His next words soon remedied that.

She sank down into a chair and looked up at him, holding his gaze until he realised she was serious, that she would not back down. Then he leaned against the table and folded his arms, sighing impatiently.

"You cannot go to court and announce yourself as the Countess of Summerville because as far as the Queen and all the court is concerned, the Countess is already in residence."

She had no idea what she expected him to say, but it certainly was not this. She was too shocked to speak for a few moments, but it seemed he was not going to continue without some prompting.

"What does that mean, exactly?" She asked at last.

"There is a woman," he began reluctantly, "Lady Rachel Stewart. Richard presented her as his Countess after Alicia's birth and she has been there ever since."

She was shaking her head, unable to believe any of this tale. Her heart twisted when she thought of her husband living in the palace with another woman; it twisted more when she realised how much he must love this Rachel, to risk so much to keep her close to him.

She relived for a brief moment his tender lovemaking and that memory gave her a small hope.

"You lie!" she cried. "I do not believe any of this. The Queen has met me; she knows who I am."

"She has poor eyesight and Lady Rachel resembles you a lot. You cannot expect that she would remember you after so short an acquaintance. Her most trusted advisor is saying the woman is his wife; why should she doubt him?"

"Am I supposed to be flattered?" she demanded as she jumped up and faced him. "Am I supposed to believe he is bedding her because she reminds him of me?"

She felt her voice rising and could not stop it, even though Anthony looked uncomfortable.

"Hardly. He has known her for many years; she was his mistress long before he ever met you."

So this was why she had not been invited back to court. This was the reason the Queen had not insisted; she believed Lady Summerville was there already. And this woman, whoever she was, was risking her own life to take her place, to impersonate her. Why? Because the Earl asked her to, that was why. So she must love him very much and he must love her in turn, to risk his life to keep her close. From another's viewpoint, it would be a beautiful love story. From Bethany's, it was the worst betrayal.

"Why did he not marry her then?" She demanded bitterly.

"She is twice widowed and has never borne a child. Richard would never marry a woman who has proved herself barren."

It was the final straw. He had loved another woman but had married Bethany for an heir, and had even disclosed his intention to carry on seeing her. Why had she not seen it all this clearly before? Why had she fooled herself into thinking that he cared for her?

Had he chosen her because she looked like his whore? And had he chosen a commoner so that she would be grateful enough to tolerate any sort of insult?

"My God!" She cried angrily. "But I do not know this man of whom you speak! He is openly carrying on an affair with his whore? He is two different men, the one he presents to the Queen and the one he brings home to me. He must think it the greatest good fortune that I prefer to be here at Summerville Hall than at court. He comes back merely to make a son. I knew it the last time."

She could feel the tears begin to gather, making her eyes sting, but she would not weep before this boy; she had to get away.

"You do see why it would not be safe?" Anthony was saying worriedly.

She did not reply, only spun around and raced up to her bedchamber. She needed to think, and she needed privacy to sob away the pain which was breaking her heart.

She closed her eyes and searched her memory for his words when he proposed their marriage. *I have mistresses and I intend to keep them.* That is what he had said and she had chosen to forget it. But there was a huge difference between many mistresses and just one, one whom he would risk his safety, his very life for. And was her first attraction for him only that she resembled her? She was second best; she was but a poor shadow of his real love and every time he bedded his wife, he thought of his mistress. She looked like her, so he could open his eyes when he made love to her and see his trollop!

Those first few weeks, quietly alone with him at Summerville, had been the happiest of her life and she had not expected them to change. Now it was all different; now he was arch enemy to the many Protestants still in England, while keeping a whore who no doubt felt the same. And if the Queen found out she was not his wife, that he had lied to her face, it would be considered treason. It would indeed mean his death. The woman meant so much to him he would risk his life to keep her close? It was little wonder he had been so unhappy that Bethany had fallen in love with him – he knew she would be hurt, badly hurt. At least the man had that much compassion in him.

She had believed for a little while that he loved her as she loved him. Now she could see the man she loved had never really existed at all and she had been fooling herself in the worst possible way. From that moment on, she promised herself she would try to distance herself from him, try to fall out of love if that were possible. He did not want her and she was only embarrassing them both by making her affection so apparent. If only it could have been that easy.

***

Richard folded the letter from his cousin and slipped it into his pocket. So she knew. The one thing he did not want to happen, Bethany knew about Rachel. But she did not know the truth and he did not want her to.

"You are going to tell her now, Richard?" Rachel said.

He shook his head slowly.

"I think not. She is better not knowing; it will make her think less of me and that is a good thing."

She sighed impatiently.

"How can it be a good thing? She loves you, she adores you! She thinks you are living here in the palace with another woman, a woman you love enough to lie to the Queen for." She paused, put her hand on his cheek and turned his head towards her. "Do you want her to hate you?"

"Yes, I want her to hate me," he answered. "It is the only way she will not be hurt by this."

"I think it is too late for that. She is already hurt, but why would you want her to hate you?"

"If she hates me, she will not attempt to see me. She will stay at Summerville, give her love to our daughter; she will not want anything to do with me."

"If she hates you, she may want revenge. She could well come to London, tell the Queen's counsellors she is your wife. You must see her,

Richard; you must try to make her believe the truth, for all our sakes."

"No, she will not do that. Seeking revenge of that nature would endanger me and she will never do that. Besides, she agreed to my lifestyle when she accepted me. She made certain promises to me and she has so far kept none of them. I know her failure to give me a son troubles her, as does her failure to even pretend to be Catholic. She broke those promises; she will want to keep this one."

Rachel bit her lip in frustration.

"You are a fool, Richard!" She said, turning away from him. "You believe a woman who loves you as your wife loves you will stay quietly miles away while you bed another woman? Sometimes I fear for your sanity."

***

Despite knowing her husband was not faithful, despite knowing what he really was, Bethany still hoped he would be home for Christmas. But that would not be possible, would it? Not unless he sent his whore off somewhere else. She lie in bed at night and longed for him, just like before. She could close her eyes and recall his touch on her skin, his lips on hers, that passionate kiss that only he could give, and she could not accept the truth; there had to be some mistake. But rack her brains though she tried, she could think of nothing which would explain his behaviour, except that he really had meant it when he said he had no intention of being faithful. Why should she think he had not meant it? He had meant all his other conditions, so why single that one out? She had to accept it: he did not love her, he had never loved her, he loved someone else, another woman who Bethany resembled.

But she would still be prepared to share him, if he would only come home for a little while and she hated herself for that. Richard would loathe that weakness, even if it were in his favour.

She was left alone at Christmas. There were no important people to entertain, no minstrels playing music, no husband to accompany her to midnight mass. Even Anthony had gone away, gone to France where he had a younger sister living in a convent. His wife knew about his whore now, there was no longer a need to pretend; now he could celebrate his Christmas where he wanted to, with his Queen and his trollop.

There was no one but a few servants for company and her little Alicia. She loved it, all the excitement, the lighting of the Yule log, the gathering of holly and hanging it inside the house. Her eyes sparkled with joy, joy that Richard should have been there to see and to share.

Bethany took gifts of meat to the people on the estate, just as she had last year though then Richard had been at her side. She was getting more proficient at horseback riding, but she still felt happier with a companion. Today it was Alicia's nurse, as she took her little daughter with her, sitting astride her saddle before her, and the women delighted in speaking to her.

"Oh, but she has grown so much, My Lady," one woman exclaimed. "She is looking more and more like you every day. Pray God, one day soon she will have a brother to resemble your handsome husband."

She meant no harm by her words, but they cut through Bethany like a knife.

One woman who answered her cottage door wore a hood half over her face, despite having come from inside. She wondered if she had enough wood for her fire, if it were cold inside. That would need to be remedied at once; Richard would not like that. But when her hood fell back, she saw that the woman had severe bruises down one side of her face, her eye was swelling rapidly and her jaw was stiff when she spoke.

It was then that Bethany remembered who she was and the conversation Richard and she had had about her that very first day.

"What has happened to you, Mistress?" She asked her gently.

"I fell, My Lady," she replied quietly, trying to cover her face. "I am so clumsy."

She did not believe her.

She dismounted and lifted Alicia from the saddle, passing her to her nurse. "Take Lady Alicia back to the Hall please."

When they had gone she turned back to the woman.

"Did your husband do this to you?" She asked.

Again she pulled the hood further over her face.

"No, My Lady," she said, though it was clear she was lying. "I fell."

"I do not believe you, Mistress. You know His Lordship would not tolerate this sort of abuse."

Still she shook her head, and there was nothing more Bethany could do. She could hardly force the woman to make a complaint, and to be honest she had no idea what Richard had threatened the man with. She also wondered how many times this had happened since he told her about it; perhaps the man thought he could take advantage of Richard's absence to abuse his wife.

She did tell Anthony about it though, when he got back from his trip.

"Little Connie?" He said when she told him which cottage it was. "It is not the first time. Richard has warned him before that it will not be tolerated." He sighed and leaned back thoughtfully in his chair. "He must be stopped before the woman is dead. She knows she has only to report it to Richard."

"But he is not here is he? Perhaps that is why it has started again."

"You could be right, but I am here. She knows where to come."

"She will not admit it," She told him. "She insists she fell. She is afraid of him and afraid of what will become of her should he lose his position on the land."

"She will be cared for, make no mistake. Leave it to me."

She was silent for a moment, bringing her thoughts back to his journey to France, where he had been visiting a sister he had not seen since she was a child.

"Was your journey a successful one, Anthony?" She asked. "Is your sister well?"

"She is, thank you for asking. She has, however, decided to stay in France. She will take the veil and I think it would be the best thing for us all, but she wants to visit before then. I shall have to see what Richard has to say about it."

He said no more about either his sister or Connie's husband, but the next day, the man's body was found in the lake in the grounds. He stank of drink and had a wound to the head. It looked as though he had fallen and banged his head while drunk, then fallen into the water and drowned. Coincidence? She thought not. But she was astonished that Anthony would order such a thing.

"It was Richard's orders," he told her when she asked. "He told me that if it ever happened again, he was to be disposed of. I don't think he meant sent away with a purse of gold coin."

Then he went back to his work as though the man's death had merely been an inconvenient incident in the day's work.

"But what of his wife? What will become of her?"

"She is working in the kitchens," he said without looking up. "Since she has no children, I was able to employ her and give her quarters in the house."

She watched him working for a few minutes, then turned and left the room. Anthony was no longer a boy, that was plain. The responsibility of running things had made him grow up quicker than perhaps he would have. She felt sad at this realisation somehow, as though she had lost a little brother. Perhaps His Lordship would not need an heir after all which was as well, since he was unlikely now to return to his wife's bed.

***

Bethany's world had shattered. She had failed to give her husband an heir, failed to follow his faith, she could not fail to tolerate his mistress as well. Not that there was much she could do about it; anything she attempted to establish herself in her rightful position would result in terrible danger to Richard and that she would never risk.

So the weeks went by and every night she cried herself to sleep, thinking of his tenderness being given to another woman. He had kept his part of the bargain, he had given her access to his wealth, he had given her his title, his lovely home; if he had not given himself, well, that had not been part of the bargain, had it?

She had little to do but enjoy her little Alicia and realise with sorrow that her father would not see her first little footsteps, her first words. She was all her mother had to live for. She heard nothing from Richard; she had to accept the truth, that if she meant anything to him at all he would have tried to explain. Obviously, she meant nothing.

She worried about the fate of her parents and wondered often if they had made it to France, if more Protestants were escaping Mary's tyranny the same way. She feared the impending birth of the Queen's child, a child who would keep England under the yoke of Rome.

She thought of Julia and her little son, a son who should have been hers, and she cursed the day she had sought her out. Had she never found Julia, had she never told her about Richard's true role, she would never have discovered his true love. She would have been blind to the truth, but content to live a lie. Now she no longer had that lie to cling to.

But at the back of her mind, causing her little darts of pain whenever she thought of her, was this mistress her husband had taken to replace her. Anthony had said she looked like her, but she needed to see that for herself. Part of her still did not really believe it, would never believe it, not until she had seen with her own eyes. She intended to go to London. Not to court, as that would be foolhardy, but to London. If she watched discreetly she might see precisely who this creature was, but she had to wait until Anthony was absent. She wanted to be well on her way to the capital before he had a chance to miss her and send word to Richard.

She would visit with old friends of her parents. There were still some in London who had recanted in order to keep themselves alive. The promised birth of the Queen's child had not happened. It was August and suddenly she reappeared in public with no baby, and no sign of any pregnancy.

Her enemies were saying she had made the whole thing up, pretended to be with child in order to keep Philip at her side. Others saying she was so desperate for a baby it had caused her body to swell. She herself was saying the Protestants had bewitched her, had cursed her womb to leave it barren. God was angry because she was being too lenient with the heretics. There would be many more burnings. Even the Prince of Spain was said to be disillusioned with her increased efforts to stamp out heresy and was leaving.

And yet, Bethany's husband followed her, even while her own husband deserted her.

She managed to get a message to friends of her father begging a place to stay while she visited. Although they would not approve of her because of whom she had married, they would be too afraid to say so, especially in writing. So she was able to stay in London for as long as she needed to.

It was apparent when she arrived that her hosts did not welcome her, but she was in no mood to care very much. She was too much of a threat for them to refuse her anything, and she thought it best they remain in ignorance of her true loyalties. This way, they would do whatever she wanted.

She had come for one reason, and one reason only: to spy on her husband and see for herself what this woman had which was worth risking so much for. She was angry, angry with him and angry with her, and she hoped she could keep herself under control if she did see them.

She had brought with her a manservant from Summerville, a man named Thomas who had worked for the family since he was a child and was loyal. It would not be seemly for a woman of her position to be seen on the streets alone, even if it were safe. But the streets of London had never been safe, even less so now. She did not tell Thomas in advance where they were going, as she expected he would tell Anthony about her visit, and Anthony would definitely send word to Richard.

She had travelled by one of the Summerville carriages, but not one that was regularly in use. This one was inconspicuous, being white and having no crest or coat of arms on the doors.

She waited outside the palace, but a distance away, watching for any sign of the Earl. Thomas was obviously wondering why they were there, but he knew it was not his place to ask. She could feel his eyes on her as the afternoon went on, as the hours passed with no sign of them moving, but she refused to demean herself by explaining.

The sight of Whitehall Palace with its many elaborate carvings, its endless windows and doors, its formal gardens, reminded her of the last time she had been here, at the coronation. That was her one chance to prove to Richard that she could keep her promise, her one chance to show him she cared enough to put on a display of loyalty to the mad fanatic, and she had thrown that chance away. Just like the commoner she was born, she had not realised how important it was to him.

Eventually, she ordered the driver to take them back to her lodgings while Thomas looked at her curiously, no doubt wondering why they had sat outside the palace all day. But she did not have long to wait the next day before she saw a carriage she recognised driving toward the park, a huge black carriage bearing the Summerville crest on its doors.

She ordered the driver to follow it, at a discreet distance, and saw Thomas poke his head quickly out of the window to see what they were following. Still he said nothing; it was not his place.

At last they stopped and she looked out to see the Summerville carriage had stopped beside the lake, its occupants clearly visible from their vantage point. Inside sat a breathtakingly beautiful woman with dark hair and wearing elegant clothing. Opposite her sat Lord Summerville, laughing at some remark she had made.

Bethany watched helplessly as this beautiful woman stole his love away, bit by bit, and there was nothing she could do to stop her.

Her throat began to throb with the pain of such a sight and she cursed herself for coming at all. Why did she want to see for herself how happy he was in the company of this woman?

Tears began to flood down her cheeks as she sat, clenching her fists in fury. The need to leap from the carriage, to run to Richard and his concubine, to lash out and tear at them both with her sharp fingernails was overwhelming. She knew well that if she did not leave now, she would not be able to stop herself. And then what would he think of her? More to the point, it would not go unnoticed if Lord Summerville and his 'countess' were attacked in the park by an angry madwoman. The Queen would want to know why, Bethany would be arrested and it would all come to light. She knew all these things, yet still she could not move.

As if he had read her thoughts, Thomas ordered the carriage turned back. She smiled gratefully at him; she would gather her belongings and head straight back to Suffolk. But as they drew near to Smithfield, the carriage came to an abrupt halt. She looked out to see what the hold up was, only to be met with the sight of a huge crowd of people trudging along in front of them.

"What is it?" She asked Thomas.

He poked his head out of the window.

"It is heretics on their way to the stake, My Lady," he replied.

She was horrified, almost choked on an escaping sob.

"Coachman, get us out of here quickly."

The coachman bent down to look inside the carriage.

"I can go no faster, My Lady. This could take hours."

So she could do nothing but sit and listen to the roaring crowds, to smell the stench of burning flesh and to wish she was anywhere but here.

After half an hour or so, she once more looked out, hoping to see the crowds dispersing, but instead the sight which met her eyes almost stopped her heart. She saw just ahead a cart full of standing prisoners, their hands bound behind their backs, moving slowly to where new stakes were being hammered into the ground, new faggots were being stacked around them. One of the figures was a woman, a woman with thick, blonde hair sparkling in the sunlight.

Bethany let out a cry. She did not think anyone else had hair like that.

"Julia," she whispered, her hand going to her throat.

It could not be, could it? She was safe at the farm in Suffolk, that Charles person was looking after her, she had said so. What was she doing here, among these poor souls about to burn? It could not be her, could it?

"My Lady?" said Thomas quietly.

She flung open the door and jumped down into the street, while he called after her. She heard his footsteps running behind her, trying to catch up, but she could not stop. She found herself in the middle of a heaving crowd of stinking, sweaty bodies, trying to catch up with the cart. Thomas was right behind her and grabbed her arm, pulling her back towards the carriage while she fought to shake off his grip.

"Let go of me!" She cried. "Julia!"

The figure turned and looked down at her then and there was a look of contempt in her eyes. Bethany would never forget that look for as long as she lived.

Once more she felt the man's hand gripping her arm.

"My Lady, come away."

"But, my sister," she cried, wondering desperately what she could do to save her.

"You do not want to join her, do you?"

For the first time she looked around to see the curious stares she had attracted and realised that Thomas was right. She was putting herself in terrible danger, there was nothing she could do, nothing at all, and Julia had turned away from her.

As the bags of gunpowder which were hung between the legs of the condemned began to explode, the air filled with a choking stench which failed to conceal the smell of burning flesh. Bethany kept her eyes fixed on Julia, as though she was powerless to look elsewhere, and was still watching her as she was pulled down from the cart and tied to the stake. The faggots were lit and her eyes closed, her lips moved in silent prayer. Bethany stared as her skirt caught fire and only the explosion from the gunpowder bag drowned out her screams.

Thomas dragged her back to the carriage and pushed her inside.

It was some two hours before the carriage could move and all that time she was numb with shock. They had sat and waited while the condemned screamed in agony, while she covered her ears to no effect and while she relived that look of contempt in her sister's eyes. She hated her! With her dying breath she hated her. Julia was giving her life for her beliefs and Bethany had sold those same beliefs for wealth and power. Of course she hated her! What else should she do?

As Bethany waited she remembered their childhood together, how they would play in the grounds of her father's country house or in the small garden of his London residence, how they grew up thinking that the Catholics were a thing of the past and could never hurt them. She recalled Julia's wedding day, how beautiful she had looked and how she had kissed her and thanked her for being there.

She recalled her whispered conversation with Lord Summerville when he entered her house unexpectedly. My God! She had been trying to tell him then about the baby, but Bethany had interrupted and for no better reason than curiosity. It was so important that Julia tell him, but she had made it so he never knew, and because of her she had fled, because of her she had ended screaming in agony before a loud and venomous crowd.

Then it finally dawned on her. The baby! If Julia was gone, what had happened to her son? She knew she would not rest until she had found him and ensured his safety, even though in her heart his very existence offended her.

She stayed but one more night in London, lying awake and weeping for yet another unbearable loss. She wanted Richard; she needed his comfort, but that was something she would never have again for he was happy with the enchantingly beautiful Rachel. She had lost him, if she ever had him, and now Julia was gone as well. She had no one now, no one who would care if she lived or died, no one except a pretty little baby girl who could not yet form a sentence.

The following day, still in a state of shock and unable to focus on anything but the awful sight of her sister's death, she returned home, where she found many men arguing urgently in the great hall. Anthony was trying to reason with them, but the voices just got louder. She was far too distraught to even notice what was being said so she stood behind the screen until they had gone, until she could make her way through the hall and upstairs.

"Where have you been?" Anthony demanded as soon as she appeared.

She stopped and looked at him and felt a little smirk form on her lips. She was drained of all emotion after her ordeal and she was in no mood to appease him.

"One day, Anthony," she assured him, "you will wake from this fantasy you cherish. You know, the one that makes you think you have a right to question me."

He looked angry, something she had never seen before, but his anger had no affect on her. She was sure nothing would ever again have an affect on her.

"You've been to London?" He demanded. "Despite my warnings, you have been to see Richard."

He looked as though he might strike her, he was so angry and he looked frightened. She saw that his fists were clenched and stiff as though he were trying to control his anger.

"You need not worry," she told him. "I did not show myself at court and I was careful to avoid anyone who might have a better memory and clearer eyesight than the Queen."

He sighed with relief then leaned back against the table.

"You did not see him?"

"Oh, yes, I saw him," she replied with a bitter laugh. "I saw him riding in the park, deeply enthralled with a rather beautiful trollop. I suppose I should feel flattered that you think I resemble her." She cast her eyes toward the door where the men had retreated. "What was the row all about?"

"The Summerville church has been broken into," he replied. "The statues have been destroyed. Father O'Neil is dead."

"Dead? You mean he has been murdered?"

She was shocked and a little upset. Despite his piety, she had liked the little priest. He had been very patient with her misgivings, though he could not have known just how deep they went.

Anthony was shaking his head. "It is more likely he died of shock. He was found in the church, so he was probably in there praying when the vandals broke in."

Everyone on this land and for miles around was Catholic. It would not have been a local attack.

"Who would do such a thing?"

"Carlisle and his merry men, I should think."

"Charles Carlisle?" She asked, then once more wished she could gather back the words. Why could she never think before she opened her mouth?

Anthony was nodding. "You know him?" He asked suspiciously.

"No, of course not. I have heard the name that is all."

"I cannot imagine where."

"People talk. I listen."

He seemed to take this explanation under consideration for the time being, though she was not fooled into thinking he really believed her. She was very glad she had had this conversation before riding off in search of Charles Carlisle and a little boy named Simon.

"When will another priest arrive?" She asked, hoping to change the subject.

"I think it best that the church is sealed off for the time being. You and I can worship in the village, along with the rest of the household. If the church is repaired it will only happen again, until Carlisle and his heretics are captured."

And then what will happen to little Simon? She thought silently. Will she be the only one left to care for him? She could not bear the thought, but she had to do something for Julia, something to keep her from hating her, even though it was too late for this world.

She was forced to wait until the excitement of the vandalism had died down and Father O'Neil had been buried with the honours of a martyr, before she could go in search of her nephew. If Charles was as important as Anthony had implied, she could not afford to be seen pursuing him and she knew no other way to find the child.

She set out as soon as Anthony had ridden off to visit the farms on the estate. She was quite certain the servants were watching her every move, but they would not be in a position to follow her, so it did not really matter. She thought it likely that Anthony was still afraid she might take herself to court and put Richard at risk.

She dare not take anyone with her, so she braved the quiet roads and forest paths alone. It was the first time she had ridden out on a horse without company. That was frightening in itself.

She followed the trail she had taken before to the remote farm where she had discovered her sister, but it seemed to be deserted. She dismounted and looked into all the empty cottages, her heart sinking. There was no sign of anyone; it looked like they had all fled or been arrested, she hoped the former. She climbed back into the saddle and was just about to leave when she noticed a figure standing at the doorway of the main farmhouse, his arms folded as he watched her suspiciously. It was Charles.

"What brings you here, My Lady?" He asked angrily as she approached. "Your husband has done untold damage to my family. Does he now send you to finish us off?"

"No!" She cried, shaking her head. She stayed mounted, feeling safer and knowing she could ride off quickly if the need arose. This man was angry, his demeanour threatening and he did not believe she had not been sent by his enemy.

"Julia is dead. She told me what you did for Summerville's wealth and title; I hope you are content with your dirty bargain."

"I know she is dead, Sir," she answered bitterly. "I watched her die."

His expression softened suddenly and he took one step toward her, then he offered his hand to help her down.

"You can dismount, My Lady," he said quietly. "I will not harm you if indeed you speak the truth."

She got down, more as a sign of good faith than with any feeling of confidence.

"I promise you, Mr Carlisle," she said swiftly, "I have not seen His Lordship in many months. I came to enquire about the child, to be sure he is safe for Julia's sake. That is all."

He seemed to relax a little then and indicated that she should enter the house, but she shook her head. She had no wish to see the little boy, only to be sure of his safety.

"I will care for him, you may be sure of that. It is what she would have wanted. He is safe with me, so long as his father never learns of his existence."

His father? She wondered then how, if he had ever laid eyes on the Earl, he could have any doubt as to the identity of Simon's father. Perhaps he had not seen him, perhaps it was as Julia believed and he thought the child Sir Geoffrey's. Would he continue to care for him if he knew whose child he he? He must have read her thoughts because his next words confirmed he was not as ignorant of the facts as Julia had believed.

"I know he is Lord Summerville's son," he said, "if that is what you are concerned about."

"You know?"

"Of course. I am not blind, but his parentage is hardly the child's fault and I love him as I would love my own. I will not blame the child for his birth, you can be sure of that." He watched her for a few minutes, perhaps wondering if she had more to say. "I think it rather divine justice that the only son of the arch Papist should be raised as a Protestant."

Despite her efforts to distance herself emotionally from her husband, she was offended on his behalf.

"I hope you have purer reasons for raising the boy than to avenge yourself on Richard," she said angrily.

He gave a small, self deprecatory laugh.

"You have every right, I suppose, to suspect me of that. But rest assured, that is not my motive. That is merely a bonus."

She realised suddenly that in telling him she had not seen her husband, she had said too much. He may well know that Richard was believed to be at court with his wife. Would he use this information against him? Of course he would, but she had no way to stop him. It was better not to draw attention to her mistake.

"Tell me one thing, Sir," she began. "What had Julia done to become so prominent? You are here, you have survived. What did she do to draw attention to herself?"

"She was discovered helping a group of Protestants to flee to the coast."

Just as her mother told her in her letter, the letter which Richard had found and told her to burn. Was it possible that her carelessness had caused all this? Was it possible he had returned to London with the information after all? How was she to guess, when she did not know the man at all?

"And it was you and your people who vandalised the church at Summerville, in retaliation?"

He nodded.

"Petty, was it not?" He said. "It was a personal revenge and not one I had any right to involve my people in. I am sorry about the priest though. He seemed a harmless little man."

She felt a wave of relief at his words. He was not as ruthless as she had believed. The idea started to form in her mind suddenly, without any prior thought. Who would have believed when she set out to find her nephew that she would even have the courage to suggest it? She thought of nothing but Julia, of erasing the hatred from her eyes as she waited to meet her death. She wanted only to do something which would please her, something to bring back the love they once had for each other.

"The church will not be repaired," she said quickly before she lost her nerve. "Not yet anyway. There is a little cottage in the forest just next to it and there is an underground passage from the house to the crypt." Charles stood frowning at her. "Can we not do something with that?" She went on. "Can we not use it to help more Protestants out of England?"

Once more she had spoken without thought only this time she had no desire to grab back the words. Her sister had died for her beliefs, the Protestants needed more help, and it was within her power to help them. Who knows? She might just help Julia to rest in peace and look down from Heaven with a fond smile for her sister instead of the contempt she had displayed at the end. These were the things Bethany thought about when she made her suggestion, nothing else. She wanted to do her part for the cause, just as Julia had done. Only she did not intend to end up like her.

CHAPTER SEVEN

Her idea had been to re-open the east wing of the Hall. It had been closed for many years and needed thoroughly cleaning as well as renovating. Nobody would question it, not even Anthony. Richard would not begrudge her the funds, Anthony knew that as well as she did, and as far as he was concerned it kept her busy and kept her mind off her sister's death and her rival, Lady Rachel Stewart. He did not have to be ever vigilant lest she take off to London again and risk his cousin's life in so doing.

But she needed many servants to help with the renovations. It was an enormous task and people came and went from the village, or so Anthony believed. It was extra money for the local people, it was work they could share and nobody would take any notice if a different team turned up from time to time. Nobody who mattered would notice the servants anyway. It was a perfect plan.

Charles was suspicious when she first suggested it. He did not trust her; he believed it to be some trap and he had every right to think so. Oh, how the Earl would have loved to capture him!

"He will know," Charles objected. "Do you realise what will be become of us? It is too dangerous, for our loyal Protestants to be evacuated right under his nose."

But he grinned a little at the idea.

"How will he know?" She argued. "The priest is dead and will not be replaced. The church will be abandoned; the cottage is already abandoned. It will be the easiest thing in the world for my helpers to get to the church through the underground passage. No one will be watching, not in the middle of the night. It is far enough away from the house to go unobserved even in daylight, and is well hidden by trees."

He began to rub his hands together in glee. He liked the plan, but she was a little disturbed by his relish at the idea of helping Protestants by using the house and property of their enemy. To use Summerville Hall, that Richard loved so much, for the purpose was the ultimate betrayal, but she had not thought of that until Charles pointed it out. She felt disloyal, felt like the worst traitor. But was it any worse than what he was doing to her, living in the palace with his whore, pretending to everyone she was his wife?

That was that then – she had no chance now to repair the damage, to keep to her bargain, dirty bargain though it was.

She wondered only fleetingly just what had possessed her to think of this plan. If anyone had asked, she would not have been able to explain. Was it knowing that Richard loved someone else and always would, loved her enough to risk everything for her? Or was it that look of sheer contempt in her sister's eyes, even as she went to her execution. Even then she showed Bethany how much she hated her.

It took a few days to organise things and while it was being taken care of, Bethany made her own preparations, and those included gathering belladonna from the woods where it grew, if one knew where to look. She intended to keep a little pouch of the lethal berries with her at all times; if she were captured, she had no intention of spending her last moments screaming in agony.

She tried to sleep during the day to make up for the night's activities, but it was never easy. She could not rest; she needed to supervise the renovations, to be sure they were not interfered with.

After a days work on the east wing, the people would retire to their straw mattresses on the floor, ready to begin work again the next day. What nobody realised was that in the early hours of the morning, they would be replaced by a new crew, escorted through the underground passage to the church and then into the little cottage in the woods where they would be questioned and their identity established. They would be given funds and sent by coach to Ipswich, where small boats waited to take them to France.

The man Charles had sent to be sure there were no spies was very thorough and very ruthless. His name was Martin; he was a tall, big built, working man whose only thought was to help Protestants. Any spies found amongst them would wish they had never come face to face with Martin.

He did not trust Lady Summerville, of that she was certain, and it was only Charles' influence that kept him from doing her harm. He could not understand how the wife of the Earl of Summerville, of Mary Tudor's right hand man, could possibly be on his side. And even while he wanted to believe, he did not approve of a woman going against her husband, even if her husband was a hated Papist.

At her waist hung a purse full of coin which would be dispensed to those who needed it; Richard's coin. There was another purse, a leather one, which also hung from her waist. She had seen Martin eyeing it suspiciously before – he seemed to look at everything suspiciously – but this night he asked about it.

"What do you think it is?" She asked him.

"Who knows? A weapon, maybe."

"Of a sort," she replied thoughtfully. "It is belladonna."

"Belladonna? For what purpose?"

"It is my insurance lest we get caught. You are welcome to help yourself should the need arise." He was staring at her as though she had lost her mind. "I watched my sister die by fire, Martin. It is not a fate I intend for myself."

His expression softened and for the first time Bethany felt he was beginning to trust her.

"You are a Countess," he said quietly. "You are of the nobility and would go to the block."

"Do you think so? I have heard the decision would be for my husband to make."

"But he would not, not his own wife surely? Much as I hate the man, I cannot believe him capable of that."

"Why not? He owes me no favours, especially now. It is a risk I will not take. Should the worst happen, the poison will be offered to anyone who wants it."

"You say that as though you were offering fine wine."

"It could be fine wine in the wrong circumstances."

Did she mean it? Did she really think Richard would condemn her to the flames given the choice? Who knows but he might think he was sparing her the fires of hell. It is what the Papists believed, so she had heard, that by suffering death by fire, the heretics would be spared the torture of flames in Hell.

Martin and Bethany did not have to trust each other, or even like each other, but after this talk she felt safer in his company. They had only to work together to get these small groups to the coast and out of England.

They could not risk larger groups or someone at the house would become suspicious, but it meant every night she was in the little cottage till just before dawn making sure these poor wretches got away safely.

It was the worst year of her life as she suffered from exhaustion and even in the summer it was freezing in the little priest's cottage. Each night she would leave her warm bed and go to the east wing where Protestants were waiting; she would lead them along the tunnel which led to the crypt of the church, she would tell them what was expected of them and what they needed to do. She missed Richard, thought constantly about what he might be doing at court and her heart still ached even after a year. Each night she felt more disloyal, each night she told herself firmly that she owed him no loyalty while knowing well that she did.

She could have no idea then that worse was to come, much worse.

She was exhausted and very tetchy when after the year of success, of no mishaps at all, Martin came into the cottage from the church, dragging behind him by her wrist a lovely young girl in fine clothing.

"She is a Papist!" He declared.

Bethany could not believe what she was hearing. Anyone less like a spy she could not imagine. The girl was little more than a child, and she was terrified.

"Why do you think she is Catholic, Martin?"

"She is French."

"There are French Protestants, you know."

"I do know, and I also know that while the King of France is happy to help our Protestants, just to annoy the Queen, he is still persecuting his own. So, tell me why a French Protestant would be so anxious to return to France. Then there is this!"

She gasped in horror and reached out a hand to stop him as he shoved his great hand into the girl's bodice and came out with a huge crucifix on a chain.

"Leave us, please," Bethany told him. She was not convinced this girl was any danger to the cause and she needed to be sure. This Catholic symbol was proof he was right, she was indeed a Papist, but a spy? She doubted it.

"Why? So you can let her go?" He asked angrily.

"Martin, whatever else I might need you for in this venture it is not to undermine my authority. Leave us. Now."

She sat the girl down and took her hand.

"Well," she said gently. "Is he right? Obviously you are Catholic, but what are you doing here and why are you among this group of loyal Protestants? You surely realised how dangerous that would be."

"I had to get away," she murmured quietly. "I heard from my servants about people helping Protestants to get to France and I thought it would be my only chance to get back to my family. I should have left the cross behind, but I could not. I felt that I would have no protection without it." She gave a little grin. "Ironic, eh?"

She spoke perfect English with only a tiny hint of an accent, which was just as well since Bethany's French was sadly lacking.

"What do you need to get away from? You are only a child. What is your age?"

"Fourteen."

"And your family is in France? Why are you here?"

"I was sent here to be married," she replied quietly. "It is my husband I need to get away from. I do not expect you to understand nor to approve."

If only she knew!

"Is he unkind to you? Is he violent?"

"He is a deviant. He has damaged me in ways I am too ashamed to reveal."

"Forgive me. I shall need more than that if I am to persuade Martin to allow you to travel with the others."

She looked uncomfortable and very embarrassed, then she removed her cloak and slipped the shoulders of her bodice down to her waist. On her back and across her breasts were the scars left by a whip. Some were healed, some were fresh and one or two were still bleeding. Bethany pulled her clothing back to where it belonged and wrapped her cloak about her. Martin was going to take her along, whether he liked it or not.

The girl flinched and drew a quick breath and a similar sound came from the doorway. Martin had been listening, as she assumed he would be. He did not trust her to make life or death decisions and she knew he always listened in, but this time she was glad of it and she could see he agreed with her.

"If you intend to send me back to him," the girl was saying, "I would prefer you give me to your Martin."

When the group had left and Bethany had heard the carts taking them away she sat before the dying embers of the fire, remembering the girl's words and feeling pleased that they had been able to help her. She smiled as she imagined the girl's husband when he found she had gone, when he realised he would have to seek out another victim.

She said a little prayer for her future before sleep overcame her.

***

Richard had toyed with the idea of going home for some weeks before finally deciding. He had not seen his wife for a year and although Rachel had stopped trying to persuade him to tell her the truth, he had begun to think himself that it might be best. He had admitted a long time ago that he loved Bethany, and his attempts to push her away had been for her own sake. But he could not bear to think of her alone and believing he loved someone else. That was selfish, because he had wanted her to think less of him and this was the ideal way to do it, but still he did not want to hurt her.

He missed her. The palace was full of beautiful women and there was no shortage of invitations, but he had no use for them, could not arouse any real interest in any one of them. The woman who appeared in his dreams each night was Bethany; she was the one who slipped her lovely body, naked and warm, into his bed in those dreams. She was the one who kissed him, held him, made love to him. There was not a woman alive who could make him feel as she made him feel and the yearning for her was almost unbearable.

Mary's fanatical campaign to rid the country of heretics was getting more zealous and Richard was disillusioned now. When she took the throne, he had been prepared to lay down his life for her if necessary, but then he had believed her when she said she wanted to convert the Protestants peacefully, without bloodshed. Now he could only look on her with disgust and he understood precisely how Bethany felt, as he found it very difficult himself to be polite to the woman. He hoped she had not noticed, for all their sakes.

And then there was the boy. Over a year ago he had gone after Charles Carlisle; he had finally found out where he was hiding, where he was organising the mass exodus of Protestants to France, and when he spied on him, wanting to see how the land lie for future reference, he had seen the boy.

There was no mistaking his heritage; it was like looking into a mirror which reflected the past. What he did not know was how and more importantly, who. He had bedded too many women in his life, but none of them of the farmer class and this child was too young to have been mothered by any of them.

He had sat on his horse for a long time, watching from a hill and hidden from view by a clump of trees. The child ran to Charles Carlisle, calling him 'father' and that word had cut through Richard like a knife. He had no son with the woman he loved, with his wife, and it seemed unlikely he ever would, and here was a child who was so obviously his, calling another man 'father'.

He swallowed the ache in his throat and watched some more. Only one woman could have mothered this boy; he knew the whereabouts of all the others. This one had run away with nothing, run away to hide when Richard had married her sister.

As if to confirm his conclusion, a figure in drab linen with thick, pale blonde hair cascading from beneath her cap, emerged from the farm house and scooped the child up into her arms. Carlisle stepped toward her and kissed her tenderly, then all three had gone inside together. She had found someone to love her at last, someone who appreciated a beautiful woman, unlike that deviant she married. She looked happy, and he was glad. He would do nothing to jeopardise that happiness.

As he turned his horse and rode away, he made a vow to protect this boy and his mother, no matter what it cost him, and he knew he could no longer pursue this man because of the child. He also remembered how Bethany had learned about Rachel, about his own position in the service of the Queen. She had found Julia, Anthony had told him, so it followed she must also have found Julia's son. The realisation made him want to forget everything else and ride home to her, made him want to explain, if explanation there could be.

He left Rachel at an inn near her Finsbury house and continued on to Summerville Hall, his thoughts focused on the best way to approach Bethany, his heart focused on making love to her again. She may not allow it; he expected resentment from her, he expected her to despise him.

Rachel had been right – he had it all wrong. He could have told her the truth, even if she would never believe it; at least it would have been better than total neglect, complete indifference. She likely believed he had not given her a thought all this time, and he was not prepared to let her go on thinking it.

When he arrived the house was dark and everyone was sleeping. He smiled as he imagined waking her with a kiss, or perhaps he would undress quietly and slip into the bed beside her so that she would wake to find herself in his arms. Would she welcome him? Had he already damaged her love too much to repair?

He opened the door to her dark bedchamber. There was not a candle alight, but the drapes were not drawn and he could see by the light of the moon that the chamber was empty. He moved to the bed, just to be sure, and found no sign of his wife. He sat on her bed for a moment to savour the lingering smell of her perfume and he smiled.

His first thought was that she had perhaps gone down to the kitchens for a drink and he got to his feet, intending to go and see, but as he passed her window he glanced out to see a light bobbing among the trees beside the church.

He watched for a long time, long enough to see more torches among the trees, long enough to see a light glowing in the church window, the same church which Anthony had ordered closed up after the death of Father O'Neil.

He went downstairs and opened the door to the underground passage, saw the torches already alight in their sconces on the walls. There was but one person who could have done this, but he did not want to believe it. When he reached the crypt he waited on the steps beneath the altar and listened while a man's voice gave instructions about a sea journey, about boats waiting to take people to France. He was about to show himself when he heard Bethany.

"Follow me," she said and he listened to many footsteps making their way towards the doors. He waited until it was quiet then he climbed the rest of the way into the church, went to the stained glass window and watched as the people made their way to the priest's cottage. A further vigil showed them leaving the cottage clutching purses and through the forest towards two waiting carts. He could guess what those purses contained; money, his money. And she was using his house, his church.

Richard stayed in the church for a long time, desperately struggling with his mounting fury. He had not seen Bethany come out of the cottage, so he waited; she would have to come back through the church to return to the house the way she came, but there was no sign of her and he was afraid to go and find her until he had himself under control.

She had not even tried to conceal her rank by hiding her clothes; she would get them all suspected, Summerville would be forfeit, they would all end in the Tower.

He had not felt this angry for many years, but now he was terrified of what he might do to her if he did not calm himself before confronting her. He had come all this way to explain, hopefully to feel her love again; to be faced with this betrayal was too much for him to bear, he would never forgive her for this.

***

Bethany fell asleep before the fire that night and when she woke the light was just seeping through the grimy screens. She wondered what time it was; it was hard to tell in this place. The trees let in little sunlight, even on a bright day, but it felt early. It was cold, though, since the fire had died and she shivered as she started to sit up.

A movement beside the door told her someone else was in the room and she looked quickly around for a weapon, but there was none. It was still fairly dark but she could see a shadow and feel a presence. She pulled herself up straight just as the shadow moved towards her. It was Richard.

Her heart jumped with fear. How long had he been here, how much had he found out? He could not have been here when the carts left, could he? Of course not, he would have stopped them. But he just stood and stared at her and his jaw was clenched in rage, his angry scowl murderous.

"Richard," she whispered, getting to her feet and desperately searching her mind for an excuse for being here.

"Are you trying to get us both killed, My Lady?" He demanded angrily, his fists clenching at his sides, and she was sure he was trying to keep from using them on her.

"What do you mean?" She lied. "I fell asleep. I came to see if anything could be done to this place, if it could be used as a home for some poor soul."

"Please, do not compound your sins by lying to me."

Bethany could not recall ever being so afraid and she began to shake, yet still the sight of him made her heart tremor with longing. She should be fleeing for her life, or begging on her knees for forgiveness, but all she wanted was to hold him in her arms, to snuggle her head against his chest, to kiss his lips. What a fool she was!

He stood staring at her, his dark eyes piercing with anger, but he remained calm, dangerously calm. She knew he had discovered what was going on, that he would now be compelled to act on the information. He was Mary's right hand, the arch papist; what would he do? Would he condemn his own wife, have her taken to the Tower and beheaded for treason. Or would he condemn her to the flames as she had told Martin he might well do. She felt for the little leather purse of toxic berries which hung at her waist.

She moved toward him, intending to hold him, but he shook his head and held up his hand to ward her off. She thought of the wife beater and wondered how many others had met their end when they got in his way. Rosemary? Her death was certainly timely. This dawn she was sure would be her last.

"Richard, please…"

Once more he shook his head, slowly, threateningly.

"Please do not speak. You can have nothing to say to me that I might want to hear."

So, she was not even to be allowed to beg forgiveness. This was the pretext he wanted to ease his conscience, to discard her and replace her with the beautiful Rachel.

Her memory showed her the two of them, laughing together as they drove through the park, and that memory made her angry. She clung to that anger to give her courage.

"So have you had your cousin spy on me, My Lord?" She asked. "Is that why you have come back?"

His mouth went down and she thought she saw regret in his eyes, but he did not answer her question.

"Here is what will happen," he said angrily. "This afternoon I shall bring the carriage to convey you to court."

To court? What was he talking about?

"What about your whore, My Lord?" She demanded.

She looked for a reaction, but he did not seem to feel it necessary to defend her honour, nor did he seem in the least ashamed that Bethany knew about her. Of course not; he had told her at the start how things would be. He had told her other things as well which she had chosen to ignore.

"Do not concern yourself with her," he replied. "You are not really going to London; that is merely what the household will believe."

She could only stare at him, feeling her heart hammering and her lips trembling but having no control over either of them. She was to climb into the carriage and then what? A convenient accident, no doubt.

"Am I then to be a party to my own death?" She said, biting back the tears.

There were just the two of them here. He could strangle her with but one of his strong hands and no one would ever know what had become of her. Why should she help him to do away with her by playing the part he demanded?

"Death?" He repeated with a frown, as though he had not understood her words. "If I wanted you dead, you would not now be breathing."

"What then? What do you have in mind for your treacherous, heretical wife?"

He stared at her for a few moments before he answered and she could see hurt behind the anger. That hurt made her realise for the first time what she had done; she had broken all her promises, had used the home which he loved to aid his enemies, and her betrayal had hurt him. Well, good, she thought. His betrayal had hurt her too, his betrayal with his trollop, but even as she thought it she knew it was unfair. He had given her everything he promised, he had nothing with which to reproach himself. He did not love her, he had never pretended to love her; was it his fault that she adored him?

He drew a deep breath then spoke at last.

"You will have your clothes packed and loaded on to the carriage," he said. "You will tell everyone I am taking you to London. But you will come here."

She looked around the place, the sparse furnishings, the mud floor, the darkness which never lifted, not even in the winter when the trees were bare. It was not as bad as it could have been had Father O'Neil not lived here, but it was far removed from what she was accustomed to. He could not mean it; he could not really expect her to live here.

"Here?" She asked, her voice shaking.

"Yes," he said. "Since you like this place so much, you may stay in it. Nobody will know you are here. As far as anyone is concerned, you are at court. Only Anthony will know you are not. It is well hidden among the trees. Before King Edward, before the church was locked up, food was left there for the poor to collect at will. It is a tradition I have been meaning to revive and now seems as good a time as any, but you will keep out of sight. I want no one to recognise you." He paused then frowned in concentration. "There will be no more fleeing heretics from this place."

Food left in the porch? No one to serve her, to cook for her? She would never survive. She bit her lip to keep from crying.

"What about Alicia?"

"What about her? She has nurses, she will be told the same story should she ask. If you go anywhere near her, she will know. She will not know to keep quiet. You will promise me?"

"No," she replied. "You ask too much, My Lord. I am her mother, she needs me. I will stop helping the Protestants, I swear it, but I cannot be kept from my child."

"You will do as I say, Madam," he insisted, then he took a step toward her and his powerful hands came to rest on her neck. She felt his heart beating rapidly, felt his fingers on her throat twitching with rage. "If anyone, anyone at all should find out who you are, I will kill you. That is a promise you may depend on." His hands tightened around her throat, not enough to choke but enough to make it hard to breathe and let her know just how easy it would be. "Had you concentrated your efforts on being her mother, instead of a heretic and a traitor, we would not now be having this conversation."

She wanted to plead with him, desperately wanted to beg his forgiveness, but she was terrified. She felt sure if she showed him weakness he would lose what little control he had over his temper and those strong hands would snap her neck like a twig. She remained silent.

"Until this afternoon, then," he said softly as he released her, but his tone was menacing.

When he had gone she looked around the little cottage and wondered how she would be able to survive, living in it all the time and with nobody for company. Her eyes wandered up to the hole in the roof where the smoke went out, at the waxed screens over the windows, at the floor of impacted mud. She thought of all those poor tenants having proper chimneys built into their homes at Richard's expense, while his wife lived with a circle of stones on the floor and a hole in the roof.

He could not mean it. He was just angry, and who could blame him? He would have changed his mind by this afternoon, he would have realised how impossible it would be. She should never have betrayed him like this but in all honesty, until this moment, she had not realised she was betraying him. She knew what she was doing was dangerous and against the law and she knew Richard would be furious if he knew, but the idea that she was betraying him, as her husband, had never really occurred to her. What a fool she was, what a thoughtless idiot.

He had done nothing to her he had not openly said he would do at the beginning, nothing she had not willingly agreed to. He had not hurt her intentionally before, had he? She did it because of Julia, because of that look of contempt in her eyes, because of her screams of agony as the flames tore at her. She did it because she was eaten up with jealousy of a woman called Rachel.

But now she had to stop thinking of herself and decide how she was going to stop the evacuation. How was she going to get word to Charles that this place was no longer safe? She could not risk even one more trip. They would even now be arriving at the house, ready to take up their places as cleaners until the evening. Her heart was hammering as she fled through the passage and up the stairs to the east wing. If Richard knew as much as he did, he would also know about them. They could all be on their way to prison right now.

When she flung open the big, heavy door, it was to find the rooms deserted. Nobody was there and she was sure she was responsible for their deaths. But there was nothing she could do; Martin would come to the cottage this evening as usual and no doubt a trap would be laid for him. And Charles? Richard had failed in his efforts to locate Charles Carlisle all this time. She could only hope that would continue.

As she supervised the loading into boxes of her clothing she knew she would have no reason to wear any of this finery and he would have no reason to keep her alive. He had chosen his whore over her, Anthony had proved himself capable of inheriting Summerville Hall and the title, so he had no need now of an heir. She would never feel his arms around her again. She would not even have her little daughter. She had made a bargain with the devil and the devil could never be trusted.

She kept her back to the servants who were packing her things so they would not see the tears brimming in her eyes. As soon as they had gone, she laid down on her bed and stared up at the canopy above her head, wondering if there were anything at all she could do to make him change his mind. The bed was elegant, the mattress and bolster soft feather and she dreaded the night to come when she would lie down on straw, low to the ground so the rats could get in, so the draught from the ill fitting door could chill her bones. She shook her head. Was she really going to submit to this? Was she really going to obey her husband's command and imprison herself in that dark and damp little hovel?

She would run away, perhaps find some safe haven away from here. Julia had found somewhere, so could she and she had money, gold coin Richard always left for her.

She got up and ran to the cabinet where the little leather casket was kept, the casket from where she had taken money to give to the fleeing Protestants. It was gone. Jewels, she had jewels. Julia had taken jewels to sell when she left Winterton House, Bethany could do the same. She opened the velvet covered box where her jewels were kept, only to find it empty. Her heart sank. He had planned it carefully, planned that she should not escape as he knew she would be too afraid to leave with no means whatsoever. And if she did he would only hunt her down and kill her anyway. She had no energy left to plan anything. She had lost everything for which she had sold her soul. She was no longer welcome in the beautiful mansion and grounds; another woman wore her title; her beautiful gowns would disappear and she did not even have the man who had promised all those things to her, the man she still adored. She had nothing left worth fighting for.

Her glance fell on the gold wedding band she still wore on her finger and the diamond ring Richard had had made for her when she gave birth to their only child. She could sell those, but she knew she would never do that. They were too precious; she could never part with those.

She chose a gown of blue velvet with a sweepingly low neckline which showed off her bosom to its best effect. She thought she may as well try to tempt him; he may change his mind if he could be made to remember what they once had.

Helplessness was not a feeling she enjoyed. It was helplessness about her future that had made her agree to a treacherous bargain in the first place, but she never expected to feel it again.

She decided to swallow her pride, get down on her knees if she had to, beg his forgiveness. She would stay in Summerville Hall, never leave the house if that is what he wanted; she could not live in that peasant's hut. But when he strode into the bedchamber he wore the same angry glare, his jaw clenched tightly, his hands still bunched into fists at his sides. She had hoped he would have calmed down by now, that he would have decided to spare her, but she could see nothing had changed. If anything, he was even angrier than he had been that morning.

"Richard, I…"

"You are ready, My Lady?" He interrupted as though she had not spoken.

She did not reply. She would never be ready for this.

He handed her into the carriage then climbed to drive the coach himself.

At the cottage, he got down and held out a hand to help her out. He took her arm to lead her toward the door. He gripped her tightly, his fingers pinching into her flesh and dragged her roughly toward the rickety wooden door.

"What about my clothes?"

"You will not be needing them," he replied.

So he was planning her death after all. What else could he possibly mean by saying she would not need clothes? She was soon to learn the answer. An old oak chest stood at the end of the bed in this tiny room. He flung it open to reveal the clothing of a peasant. "You can store your gown in here. No one must see you in it."

She made no move toward the chest, but she could see enough to know there was nothing there befitting a countess, just drab, natural linen and grey wool. He gripped her arm again and spun her round to unlace her bodice at the back, and she caught back a sob which threatened to choke her. His fingers on her back reminded her vividly of all those nights when he had insisted on sending away the servants and undressing her himself; she could not believe he was not also remembering those nights.

Once her bodice was loose enough, she shrugged herself out of it and turned to show him her cleavage overflowing the silk shift. He must want her, surely he must. After all this time, he must yearn for her. But he had Rachel; he had no need of his wife.

His jacket was open and she put up a hand and slipped it beneath his shirt.

"Richard, I am sorry," she pleaded. "Please forgive me. I wanted only to help."

He did not move, just looked down at her hand where it rested over his naked breast, and the look of contempt in his eyes matched Julia's when last she saw her. She shuddered and pulled her hand away, tears overflowing now and soaking her cheeks.

"People will ask who you are," he went on in a harsh tone. "They will be told you are the daughter of a former servant, come to seek solitude. They will be told you are suffering from leprosy; that should keep them away."

She gasped, swallowed the hurt and tried to summon some anger of her own.

"So I am to be left here, alone, people afraid to come near enough to see what I look like. What an absolutely brilliant plan, My Lord. I congratulate you!" He made no reply. "Is it your plan to drive me mad?"

"It is my plan to protect us both from your misplaced loyalties, Madam," he replied and his voice was rising rapidly in anger.

"Misplaced? I suppose I should have supported you in your efforts to help the Queen send more innocent people to the stake. Did you know I watched my sister die?" He flinched at that, obviously it was news to him. "Did you know she was dead?"

"Yes, I did, but I did not know you had witnessed it."

She could only marvel at his calm. He had been her lover, albeit only briefly. How could he talk as though she were just another heretic among many? Bethany could take no more, her frustration and anger were rising and the need to lash out was overpowering. She could not stop herself from lifting her arm and striking him hard across the face.

He caught her wrists to ward off a second blow while she cursed the tears that flowed down her face. She tried to take a step back but he held fast to her wrists; his expression was murderous and she was sure that this time he would kill her.

"My God, but you have a lot of nerve," he shouted. "You, who have broken every promise you made to me have the gall to strike me?" She struggled against him but his grip was too strong, and he pulled her roughly toward him, bringing his lips close to her ear. "One last try, darling," he whispered seductively.

"What do you mean? What are you talking about?"

"One last try for a son, I think, before I leave you."

Did that mean he did want her? Or was he merely toying with her, building her hopes of release only to let her fall. Whatever his intention, she had to try; it could be her only chance to avoid this squalid prison.

"You want me to make love with you?"

"Oh, I don't think I would call it making love exactly," he replied harshly.

Then he pushed her down roughly onto the hard floor, bruising her back as he climbed over her, pinned her to the floor by sitting astride her and unfastened his breeches. She twisted and struggled to free herself but he caught her wrists in one hand, pushed her skirt up to her waist and forced her legs apart.

She began to sob, loud, wrenching sobs escaping her while her face creased up in misery. He could not do this, not Richard. She could not believe he was doing this.

"Richard, please," she begged between sobs. "This is not you."

He did not answer, just laid his full weight on her body and pushed himself painfully into her, grazing her buttocks and the backs of her thighs on the rough surface.

"Yes," he said viciously. "This dirt floor will suit your type nicely."

CHAPTER EIGHT

After returning the Summerville carriage to the coach house, Richard went into the house to find a maidservant.

"There is a box of Her Ladyship's clothes in the carriage," he told her. "She decided to have new gowns made when she gets to London. See that they are unpacked and put away."

The maid curtsied.

"Yes, My Lord," she murmured.

If she noticed his angry mood she would make no mention of it but he felt her gaze following him as he made his way to the nursery to say goodbye to his daughter. She had grown so much since he saw her last; his plan had been to spend some time with her and her mother, but that plan was destroyed now – she had destroyed it. He could not stay here, not now, not with his treacherous wife only a mile or so away. He was tempted to take Alicia with him, but he had no idea if Rachel would be willing to play the part of a mother as well as a wife. Besides, Alicia would know she was not her mother; in her childish innocence she could give them away.

Her little arms wrapped themselves around his neck and made him catch back a sob. Did he really want to separate her from her mother? No, he did not, but it was Bethany's own doing and he could do nothing about it. The child was very young; she would soon forget her.

In the stables he saddled his stallion himself. He was in no mood to wait for a stable hand or a groom and he wanted the comfort of something whose loyalty was without question; his horse fitted that description better than anyone.

He rode away, as fast as he dared, galloping until he had put some distance between himself and that treacherous bitch. He could easily have killed her; he wanted to kill her and when he put his hands around her throat it had taken colossal effort not to squeeze and squeeze until her face turned blue and no breath remained in her. That would have given him a great deal of satisfaction. How could she do this to him? And how could he forget his own principles so far as to take her by force and so brutally?

He slowed his horse to a walk as he battled with his conscience, tried to reason with himself, to comprehend how he could have committed such a sin. He told himself she was his wife, he was entitled to her body, any time he wanted it and in any way he wanted it. But his sense of justice would never allow him to believe that and his memory would not let him forget how she sobbed, how she pleaded with him. He was disgusted with himself.

He had come home hoping for her love; he had wanted her, yearned for her, and he had still wanted her despite her treachery, despite his rage. He wanted to hurt her, he wanted to make her pay for her deceit and he had done the one thing he had always detested, he had turned the exquisite act of love into a weapon.

He would never forgive her, that was certain. He had been striving to push her away, to make her think less of him, and it seemed he had achieved his wish. She must hate him to have betrayed him like that and if she didn't hate him before, she certainly would now.

He rode slowly for the rest of the way, for the sake of his beloved horse, and stopped at an inn to refresh them both before he continued on his way back to London.

The place was crowded, being the only inn on the main road to London, but he was well known and the landlord soon found him a table away from the noise and raucous laughter, where he could think about the events of last night. He never wanted to see his wife again; she had gone too far. But he had no grounds to divorce her. He knew what he should do, what he was duty bound to do, and that was to arrest her for heresy and treason. He was still angry enough to do it, but he could not take the chance that given desperate circumstances she would speak out, announce to the world she was the Countess of Summerville.

Yet his own safety and Rachel's was not his only consideration, although his fury tried to persuade him it was. He tried to imagine

Bethany kneeling before the block, her head leaving her shoulders, or even worse tied to a stake like her sister. His heart hurt as he summoned that image. Yes he hated her now, he would never see her again, but his conscience would never allow him to live with such an act. She was his wife; should he condemn her to the block?

No, she would be allowed to live, so long as she could fend for herself like the peasant she was. He felt no shame about the living quarters to which he had condemned her; other people lived in places like that, so could she, and he had no intention of ever releasing her.

***

It was dark when Bethany finally picked herself up from the floor and dusted down her gown. It was also cold now the fire was dead and she realised with a jolt that she had never in her life had to light one before. She had no idea how to do that; he would have her freeze to death, perhaps? She moved unsteadily to the bed in the corner of the room and climbed in beneath the fur covers. A good thing Father O'Neil had lived here, or she would not even have that much.

A wave of terror tore through her then. It was nearly winter; how was she supposed to survive, living like this? She had never had to lift a finger for herself in her entire life, there had always been servants to do everything for her. She had no idea how to keep warm, much less feed herself. She still could not quite believe he meant it, that he would not calm down in a day or two and rescue her. He could not really mean for her to live like this, could he?

She had cried herself to sleep on that hard floor, her bruises growing more painful as her limbs grew stiffer and her heart was torn apart. Her face was wet and dirty; the dirt from the floor had turned to mud on her cheek because of her tears, but she hardly noticed. She could not believe he would treat her like this, to force himself on her as though she was...was what? A treacherous wife? And now she recalled vividly his warning when he first suggested their union, those words which had sent a shiver of fear down her spine. *You will not enjoy the consequences should you betray me.*

It had never occurred to her before to even consider what he had meant. He thought it unacceptable for a man to use his superior strength to intimidate a woman; she knew he would never beat her. But was what he had done any better?

When they met it was easy to make her promises, because nothing would change, because he meant nothing to her. But she had betrayed him and now she was to learn about those consequences. She had lost his respect and affection, if affection he ever had for her, and she had lost them for good.

Her wrists were turning purple where he had gripped them so tightly and she felt sore inside. She dragged up the memories of those first weeks, even though it tore her apart just to think of them, just to remember how gentle he had been, how easily she had forgotten their cold hearted agreement and fallen in love with him. And she had loved him so much, so very much. But not enough to keep her promises it seemed.

Darkness had fallen before she buried herself beneath the fur covers and slept, hoping perhaps she would wake to find it was all a horrible nightmare, sent to warn her away from her dangerous activities. Perhaps she would wake to find she had been given another chance.

The next morning she pulled the fur cover tightly around herself as she went to the dead embers of the fire and tried to recall if she had ever seen anyone light one. There had to be a way. She could not have lived all these years without seeing a servant light the fires, could she?

There were logs beside the fire and if she was going to be able to keep warm or cook something to eat, she needed to find a way to light them. In the corner of the room she found some flints and a vague memory of Martin lighting this fire came to mind. She laid it all out, the kindling, the logs and rubbed the flints together. The cold made her shiver so much she almost dropped them, but it was not only the cold which made her shake, made her teeth chatter. She was trembling still from Richard's attack, an attack she never thought him capable of. God! He must have been so angry to do that, he must have been enraged. She put a hand up to her neck, recalling how his hands had tightened around it, and she realised how lucky she was to be alive. But was this living? It was not what she was accustomed to for sure, but it was how thousands of people lived and quite happily. If they could do it, so could she.

She drew a deep breath to calm her fears and made a determined effort to rub the flints together. She was surprised and pleased when it actually worked and she managed to get a fire going.

The next thing was to remove her velvet gown and place it carefully in the chest with the clothes of a peasant. Richard had thought of everything; he had unlaced her bodice, which she would never have been able to do by herself. When he did that, she knew a spark of hope that he had amorous intentions, that she could find her way back into his heart, but he was only being practical.

She felt like a peasant, as well, as she looked at her surroundings and at the cauldron. There was nothing to eat inside the cottage, but then she could not have eaten if there had been. He said something about food being left at the church. She would have to look, unless he expected her to go out killing rabbits as well.

She wondered fleetingly how long he would expect her to stay here, if he would ever release her, find her a more comfortable prison. The way he had behaved made her think the answer was no, that he would leave her here until she died of the cold or starvation. She decided she would never see him again, that he was gone from her life for ever. But what of Alicia? He surely would want her to know her mother? Unless he now believed she was unfit to be her mother.

The mattress was straw covered in cheap sackcloth but there were fur covers to keep her warm. He hated her now, that was apparent, just as her sister hated her, as she had gone to her grave hating her. Her thoughts wandered to Rosemary; he said he hated her and the more Bethany thought about the rage he had barely been able to contain, the more certain she was that he had indeed killed Rosemary. Somehow it had always seemed somewhat of a coincidence that she should be in the middle of an outbreak of plague just when it suited him, but she had not believed him capable of such a thing, of sending her there deliberately at that time. Now she knew better; now she knew that not only was he capable, but he was quite likely to have killed her himself then covered it up by the illness. Nobody will look too closely at a corpse in a plague house.

Bethany's life was in danger, she knew that. One false step and he would dispose of her the same way he had disposed of the wife beater, or his first wife. She was not afraid of death but she could not bear to think of him doing it himself, with his own hands, those same hands that had caressed her and held her and loved her. She made sure she always had the leather purse tied to her waist, just in case.

Eventually she slept some more, though her dreams were filled with horrors. When she woke she piled more logs on to the fire, wondering briefly what would happen when they ran out. She did not think she was physically strong enough to chop wood. She went outside and up to the church doors, sealed now so that no more souls in danger could escape through them. But in the porch, as he had promised, there was food, vegetables and meat, also logs and flints. So she was not to starve after all, but it was clear he did not want her running about the place in search of sustenance, perhaps drawing attention to her presence.

It was the beginning of the end for her. Only Anthony knew where she was. She wondered what he thought about what his much loved cousin had done with his lawful wife! It mattered not what he thought; he would support Richard in all things. God punishes in His own way and in His own time and that is what He was doing now. She had little choice but to accept her fate and think about how easy it would be for him to dispose of her, now he had isolated her, kept people away with tales of leprosy. He could come in the night, or even in broad daylight, and no one would even miss her.

***

Spring came and brought beautiful colours to the trees, those colours which reminded her painfully of the first few weeks in this place, the weather grew warm and she was able to spend time walking in the forest. She found the place where they had first made love and lay down to rest there with her memories.

She had been living in that dark and dismal place for months, alone with no one to talk to. She was terribly lonely, and the lonelier she became the more she hated that damned woman her husband was keeping in his bed at the Palace. Sometimes she thought of going there, of confronting her and tearing her fingernails through that perfect face. But she was a peasant now, with no rights, and her fingernails were non existent due to the hard work and lack of nourishment. Although food was left, it was not of the best quality and her cooking left much to be desired. She would never be a grand lady again, never have that position which had cost her so dearly.

Then she heard a child's laughter and stood up, moving to the edge of the wood to see a girl, barely sturdy on her little legs, playing with a young woman whom Bethany had never seen before. It was her little Alicia. She could run now, she could laugh and she could play and her mother could do nothing but watch. And watch she did, every single day of that spring and summer she would sit at the edge of the trees, out of sight, and watch her play, listen to her laughter as the woman pushed her high on the swing.

Bethany stopped feeling sorry for herself because of her. She brightened her days and made her miserable existence worth living, and she dreaded the colder weather when she would play inside, out of sight. What was she going to do then? It was torture to watch her and not be able to wrap her arms around her and hold her close.

She had just returned to the cottage one day in late summer when she heard her name being called softly from behind the wall. She turned swiftly, wondering if she had imagined it. Nobody knew she was there, nobody save Richard and his cousin. Then a face appeared around the side of the cottage and made her start violently.

"Charles? What are you doing here?"

She took his hand and pulled him inside, looking about anxiously, afraid someone would see him, recognise him, end both their lives.

"I have been watching this place, hoping to find a way to use it again. Imagine my surprise to find you here."

"No," she replied shaking her head. "No way in the world can this place ever be used again. It would be the death of us both." She paused and looked up at him. "How are you still alive? Richard discovered me, discovered our plan. I never knew what happened to the poor souls who were waiting for the next trip out, or what happened to Martin. I suppose they are all dead."

He wore a little puzzled frown as he shook his head.

"We had word, a warning to cancel that night's evacuation and all future ones. I assumed it came from you. I knew the Earl had discovered what we were doing, I was told. I worried about what had happened to you, but when I enquired, I had word that you were living with him at court."

She laughed derisively, but she was not about to tell him the truth. He would use it against Richard, she had no doubt of that.

"I have been watching you for hours," he went on, "gathering kindling, carrying logs and food from the church door like any peasant. I could not believe it was you." His eyes swept her clothing, then looked around the cottage with a grimace. "Are you hiding, or has he imprisoned you here to live like this?" He said with a frown of disgust. "His own wife?"

"Do not fret, Charles. It is better than the alternative."

He raised his eyebrows in surprise.

"You fear for your safety?" He asked with a frown of concern. "Then do not stay. Come with me; you can help more with the cause."

She shook her head, sudden terror running through her. She had done enough, too much. She could not face it all again.

"No, Charles. I am not brave enough for that."

"But you put yourself in danger every time you send me warnings. Do you not know that? If His Lordship would condemn his wife to the life of a peasant, he would surely have no hesitation in charging you with treason."

She studied his face for a little while, wondering what he was talking about.

"Of what warnings do you speak, Charles? I know nothing about this."

"What?" He looked startled. "I have been receiving them for months now, letters usually left at the door during the night. Sometimes they have been shot with an arrow into the doorframe."

She laughed.

"I have never been proficient in archery. What sort of warnings?"

"Warnings that have saved the lives of our people. Little notes that give details of when the Queen's men are going to be in certain places, when they could have caught us all. Sometimes they have forestalled a planned trip, sometimes they are of no use whatsoever." He turned away briefly, then looked back at her. "If not you, then who?"

"I have no idea, Charles. Be sure that I have not been privy to the sort of knowledge you speak of. I have not left this place for almost a year. The Queen could be dead for all I know."

"Sadly, no," he replied, shaking his head. "I was sure it was you. Who on earth else would be doing this?"

She could think of no one who would do such a thing, no one who would be knowledgeable enough but secretly on the side of the Protestant cause.

"So will you let me take you away from this place?" Charles asked quietly.

"No," she replied. "My little girl is here. I will not leave her."

He was thoughtful for a moment before he spoke again.

"Forgive me," he said at last. "I did not know you had a child."

"Why should you? We know little about each other really, do we?"

"Then she is Simon's half sister," he said quietly. "What a very strange idea."

He pulled her toward him and held her close, not in any passionate way but as a brother might hold a much loved sister. He meant nothing to her, but just to feel the warm and comforting arms of a man again almost made her agree to go with him. Had it not been for Alicia, she would have agreed without hesitation and to hell with what Richard had ordered.

"I shall take my leave then," he murmured. "I see I am putting you in danger by simply being here. But I still have no idea who our friend at court might be."

And neither had she, but as she watched him disappear among the trees she suddenly felt bereft. It had been so good to have someone to talk to, even for such a brief time. She had not realised how much she missed human companionship. Perhaps it was Richard's plan to drive her mad, after all.

***

Once the warmer weather came life was not as bad in the cottage as Bethany had expected it to be. The truth was she was getting used to living like this and would not have suffered so much had she had something to read, or someone to talk to. She was proficient now in lighting her own fires and cooking her own food. It was a new experience and not a real hardship, when she considered what other people suffered. At least she had food, which is more than many had.

She remembered that first day when Richard had taken her to meet some of the tenants on the estate, how he had told her he was no better than them, only more fortunate. She could well understand those sentiments now. Even with her poor clothing, her arduous chores and her loneliness, she was better off than many. She wondered what her father would say if he could see her now, he who had accumulated so much wealth and had thought himself very fortunate to have acquired the hand of an Earl for his daughter. He would probably say she got what she deserved, just as she told herself. But he still would have felt embarrassed to have his daughter living like this.

She dreaded another winter though. She had never been so cold in her life as in this place through the winter. The wind blew through the gaps between the screens and the wall, the snow and rain fell through the smoke hole in the roof, putting the fire out and reducing it to smoke that choked her. She spent most of that time buried under the fur covers left behind by Father O'Neil. All she could do was pray that her husband might find it in his heart to forgive her before the next winter came. She would beg that forgiveness willingly if only there were a safe way to contact him. She dare not write, even if she had anything to write with, for fear of her letter falling into the wrong hands. No one must know she was here, he had threatened to kill her if anyone found out, and she was sure he had meant every word.

She tried to hate him, tried to despise him for what he had done to her, but in her heart she knew she still loved him. She knew if he were here, she would fall on her knees before him just for one of those warm smiles, one of those tender kisses.

She often wondered if he ever thought about her, alone in her hovel. He had enough compassion to want to keep her from being hurt, from falling in love with him; surely he could find enough compassion to remember where she was, how she was living.

At night she would awake with a start at every noise, and the forest provided many of those. She was sure the night would come when he would kill her. She had tried to obey his commands, tried to stay isolated, and she did not think anyone had seen Charles, but the day came when a female voice called from outside the window.

"Mistress," she called. "Are you there? Can you hear me?"

She peered through a gap in the waxed screen and saw the profile of the young woman she had seen with Alicia. Close up, she could see she was much younger than she had imagined, perhaps only sixteen or so. She had no idea who she was or why she had come, but she had to get rid of her. Her life depended on it.

"You must not be here, Lady," Bethany said quickly. "I am a leper. His Lordship promised he would tell everyone not to come near."

"Oh, I know that," she persisted then moved toward the door.

"No!" She cried out. "You must not enter."

"I am not afraid."

"Then you should be. Perhaps you do not understand how infectious this disease is."

"Was our Lord afraid to walk among the lepers?" She replied.

Was she likening herself to Jesus Christ? She could scarcely believe it. That was heresy even to her Protestant ears. Or was it blasphemy? It was difficult to tell at times.

"Who are you?"

"My name is Robina," she replied. "I am His Lordship's cousin, come from France."

"Anthony's sister?" Bethany said without thinking.

Robina drew a quick breath then was silent for a few moments before she spoke again.

"That is a familiar way to speak of my brother, Mistress," she said sternly.

What could she do to take back the words? There must be something.

"Forgive me, Lady," she said at once. "I meant Mr Anthony of course."

"Of course. Anyway, I came to see if you needed anything."

"No, nothing. Just to be left in peace."

"Let me come in and pray with you," she persisted. "The risk is mine."

Through the gap in the screen Bethany could see the heavy crucifix dangling at her visitor's waist, she could see the prayer book she had brought with her, a prayer book in Latin of course. Anthony had mentioned this girl briefly and she recalled him telling her how pious she was, how she would not tolerate even a hint of heresy. She wondered with what superstition she was filling her child's head, and she resented her at once.

"No, Lady," she replied at last. "The risk is mine. I promised His Lordship when he allowed me to stay here that I would have no contact with anyone. You are forcing me to break my promise and if his kin contracts this awful sickness, who do you imagine will be blamed? Not you, that is certain. He will turn me out if he finds out and I have nowhere else to go."

If only that were true, that he would turn her out. What he would do would be far worse; he had promised her that and she had no reason to doubt him. As her sister had assured her, he was a man who kept his promises.

"But he will understand," she insisted. "He will know you need to pray. What do you do for spiritual counselling, Mistress?"

Bethany had no answer for that. It had never even occurred to her that she was missing mass on a regular basis. She searched her mind to see if she knew of a leper chapel nearer than Cambridge where she could tell Robina she attended mass. She did not. Lepers would sit outside the churches sometimes so they could hear mass without coming into contact with the congregation.

"Please go, Lady," Bethany begged. "I do not wish to harm you. You will contract this disease if you stay."

"I am not afraid," she said again with a slightly maniacal smile.

"Well I am. What about that little child I saw you with? Do you realise that you could pass this curse on to her? Or does that not matter?"

She caught her breath, Bethany was not sure whether at the realisation that she was right or because of her lack of respect for her rank. She was angry. Who was she to put her child at risk just to make herself feel important?

"Very well," she said at last. "I will go. But be sure I will tell my brother how uncivil you have been to me. He will not like it, and he will be sure to tell His Lordship."

With those words she turned and ran back toward the house, leaving Bethany to wonder if she would tell Anthony. It might be the best thing, as he would prevent another visit. On the other hand, he may decide to act, to save

Richard from exposure. Her visit could be the beginning of the end, it could herald what she had feared all these months. She sat down on the bed and wept.

The following day seemed as though it might be the last of the warm days. It had begun with a damp mist in the air which would clear later, so she waited for the sun before she set out to take up her usual spot among the trees.

Alicia had come out but something was wrong. She seemed quiet today, somehow withdrawn. She wasn't running and laughing as she had been on previous days and Bethany longed to run down the meadow and grab her into her arms. There was no sign of Robina, only a nurse which made it even more tempting. Oh God, how she longed to hold her! They stayed out perhaps ten minutes, no more, then the nurse picked her up and started back toward the house with her. Perhaps she had a little fever, Bethany thought. She would be better tomorrow. But the next day she did not appear at all, nor the next. She could not bear it, not knowing. She waited all day beside the trees, hoping Alicia would appear. The weather was warm again, there was no reason for her absence.

She made up her mind then. The following day, first thing she would make her way to the house even if it was dangerous and she would not care who saw her. She had to know what was wrong with her child. That was more important than anything, even the risk to her own life.

She would go via the underground passage from the church if she could break in. She had to know what was happening, had to be sure her daughter was safe. As she walked, she began to plan how she could manage it without being seen.

But when she returned to the cottage, the familiar black carriage was waiting outside.

Bethany stood and watched, afraid to move, afraid to go closer. Why had he come? This was the result of Robina's visit, she was sure. Someone knew she was here and he had come to keep his promise. Perhaps he had taken Alicia away so she would know nothing when her mother was buried with honours.

She stood rigid for a long time, afraid to move lest she draw attention to her presence, wondering how she was going to escape without him seeing. She felt at her waist for her little pouch of berries, not knowing if she would have the courage to take the poison.

She could not decide what to do. Should she turn and run, hide among the trees, and then what? He would send a party out looking for her; she had nowhere to go. Or should she face him, put an end to the speculation and the fear she had known this past year? At least knowing once and for all would bring some relief. She was still there when he emerged from the cottage, her velvet gown clutched in his hands.

He saw her straight away; there was nowhere to hide, and he stood and stared at her for a moment, almost as though he did not recognise her, as though he wondered who she was.

"Bethany," he spoke urgently. "Come inside. You need to change at once."

What now? What devious plan had he dreamed up this time? He must have known about Charles' visit, must have sent his spies to watch her every move. So now he was about to destroy him and he wanted her for...what? And why must she change for the charade?

"Please," he persisted. "There is little time. Your daughter needs you."

CHAPTER NINE

The message from Anthony went to Richmond first. Lord knows why! Perhaps he thought Richard was there, but at any rate it was delayed and Richard was desperate to get to his daughter before it was too late.

He had so many things on his mind already, Rachel's safety being a priority. And Rachel would never have been at risk were it not for his treacherous wife. He should have made her come to court, he should have made her pretend if that is what it took. Why had he been so weak as to want to protect her and put Rachel in danger?

She mentioned that morning she was afraid the Queen was beginning to suspect and he had already noticed a change in Her Majesty's demeanour. He told Rachel to leave Finsbury and go back to Suffolk, use her own name.

This letter about Alicia made him realise he would have to face Bethany again. If Alicia were as ill as Anthony said, she had a right to be with her. He would never live with his conscience if he denied her that right.

He prayed for the child's recovery, but whatever the outcome, her mother would return to her prison. He hated her. He had tried not to think about her at all but when he had, his hatred surfaced and almost consumed him. And to think he once loved her, would have done anything for her. He expected her to hate him in return after what he had done to her and that was another reason he had no wish to face her, he was ashamed.

Perhaps to make amends for the abuse, he would find her somewhere more comfortable to live, but all he cared about now was getting to Alicia.

It was one of those rare times when he did not take the time to attend to Ebony himself. He dismounted outside the front doors and tossed the reins to a stable hand before taking the steps three at a time and hurrying to his daughter's bedchamber in the nursery wing. As soon as he saw the lesions covering her face, he knew it was hopeless. The best physicians were in attendance, as well as a priest.

"Forgive me, My Lord," the doctor addressed him. "I thought it best to send for Father Francis. I was unsure if you would arrive in time."

Richard only nodded at him. His child was dying, his sweet, pretty little girl who had meant so much to him and to her mother, and he had missed so much of her young life. And whose fault was that? If Bethany had kept her promises, they could all have been together at Whitehall. But his duty was clear: he would have to collect Bethany and bring her to the house.

He went outside and hitched up the carriage. The servants thought it odd that he insisted on driving himself, wherever he was going, but they made no comment. He told them he had to fetch Her Ladyship, but they would not ask from where.

He took the path around the trees to the front of the church so that anyone watching had no reason to suspect his destination, and as he drove toward the woods and the little hovel, he decided he would not speak to his wife unless he had to. He would tell her about Alicia, of course, but that was all. There would be as little contact as possible.

The cottage was empty when he arrived. He had no idea where she was, out collecting firewood or food he imagined, and if she did not return soon, he would have to go and look for her. It occurred to him that, after their last encounter, she could have seen the coach and decided to hide from him. He hoped not; he had no time for that.

He went to the chest and took out her blue velvet gown, the one she had been wearing when he brought her here. He shook it out to remove the creases and the dust, then he went outside to see if she were coming.

He stopped in his tracks when he saw her, standing at the edge of the trees, her eyes wide and frightened. He studied her for a moment, unsure that this really was Bethany, if this could really be his beautiful wife. She looked awful. She was almost skeletally thin, her face was pale, almost white in colour, and her hair was dull. Where had the lustre gone? Where were the glorious, thick waves through which he had run his fingers, that he had held to his face to breathe in the perfume from her soap?

All the hatred and resentment drained out of him. She looked so helpless, he just wanted to fold her up in his arms and make her better.

***

He would tell her nothing while he helped her don her forgotten finery. He stood behind her and laced up her bodice, his fingers quick and efficient, his expression forlorn. She stood still, trying not to remember when he had stood in this same place and loosened these laces, but she could not help but notice that no matter how tightly he pulled on the garment, it still hung loosely on her.

But that was of no matter now. *Your daughter needs you.* Something must be desperately wrong for him to come here, to fetch her out of her hovel to join the world, if only for the briefest time.

She could stand it no longer.

"What is wrong with Alicia?" She asked for the third time.

He turned her round and she tilted her face up to look at him, then she realised why he had not answered before. It was because he could not, because the tears in his eyes told her he could barely speak.

"She is ill?" She persisted. "What is wrong with her?"

He swallowed, then led her outside and handed her into the carriage. He climbed in beside her before he could reply.

"It is the smallpox," he said with difficulty, then he took her hand. "She is dying, Bethany. I have the best physicians to tend to her, I have prayed, but there is no improvement. I only got the letter this morning. You have a right to be with her, whatever else has happened."

"Thank you."

He left her alone and climbed down, then into the driver's seat to drive the horses himself. No one could be privy to this secret.

She lie like a little doll on the pillow, her face drawn and covered with the familiar blisters. Bethany sat on the bed and gathered her up into her arms, her little girl who she had watched so carefully, who she had not held for so long. Richard sat on the bed behind her, but he made no move to take the child from her.

It was her own fault that she had missed out on this last year of her life. Had she not betrayed Alicia's father, she might have been there to protect her. She held the small body against her, kissed the sweet face and hoped she knew her mother was with her at last.

"I am so sorry, my darling," she whispered. "I should have been with you, not helping a lot of strangers."

Tears soaked into Alicia's neck and shoulder as Bethany held her, then realised there were many others in the chamber. She had not even noticed them when Richard led her in but now she heard the chanting. It began softly and it was a few minutes before it penetrated into her mind. She looked up. There were four monks standing on the other side of the bed and they were chanting in Latin.

Fury overwhelmed her. Her child was dying and she had missed her last year because of this damned Queen and her merciless religion. She had lost her child because of it, she had lost her husband because of it and she had lost her sister because of it. And now they were here, chanting their superstitious gibberish.

"Shut up!" She screamed at them, jumping to her feet. "My baby does not need your prayers. God will receive her innocent little soul without help from you."

"My Lady," the priest said, stepping forward. "I must administer the last rites. Please."

"No! She needs no help to claim her place among the angels."

She pushed him away, but just then Alicia's breathing became ragged and she turned back to her.

Richard was behind her, catching her around the waist and pulling her away. She expected him to be angry with her and she no longer cared. Yet his voice was soft and soothing.

"Please, Bethany," he murmured. "Let Father Francis do his work."

Yes, she thought, Father Francis must give prayers to help her little one through purgatory. She believed that was rubbish but Richard did not and she was his child, too. The last thing they would ever share would be the death of their daughter. Bethany let him lead her away, although she really wanted to hold her till the end.

As they reached the door she saw Robina, standing and glaring at her furiously. As Richard guided her past, Bethany heard her mutter quietly: "Heresy".

She could not care what she thought, nor even if she had recognised her. It seemed unlikely. She had not had much of a chance to see inside the cottage; even if she had it was dark, but she might have recognised her voice. Her only concern was her little Alicia. She was gone, the only thing left worth living for, her little angel. May God protect her.

In the hallway Richard released his grip on her arm and she turned to face him, looking for signs of the contempt she had felt from him before. But all she could see were the tears, tears for their little girl. Then he surprised her totally;

he put out his arms to her and she fell into them, soaking his doublet with her own tears.

They stood like that for a long time before they moved away to the bedchamber, the one they had shared. He sat beside her on the settle, just like old times really, except he made no move to touch her.

"So she is gone," she said quietly. "The only thing left of our marriage, of our love, if love you ever felt for me."

He shifted uncomfortably, looking down at his feet as he spoke at last.

"Bethany," he said quietly. "This is not the right time, but it has haunted me for months and I have to tell you I am deeply ashamed of the way I behaved at our last meeting. It was unforgivable. I was angry, very angry, but that is no excuse for what I did to you. I have always loathed men who force themselves on women and here I am no better."

She turned to look at him in surprise; she had not expected him to apologise, not for that. He did not look up, but kept his eyes on his feet, like some naughty schoolboy about to be scolded. Finally his eyes met hers.

"Can you ever forgive me?" He said.

She had no answer to that. She had spent the past year fearing for her life, terrified that one night she would wake to find him standing over her, waiting to kill her. She even slept with the leather purse beneath her pillow, even knowing it would do no good, that there would not be time to do anything with it. And here he was asking forgiveness for *that*? Why would he? He only took what was his by right, even if he did take it brutally and leave her feeling sullied.

Her heart melted, as she believed he knew it would, but she did not reply. He was right, it was not the time as far as she was concerned. Did she forgive him? She wasn't really sure whether she did, or if she ever could. He had hurt her too much, with his whore and his scathing words, with making her live like a penniless peasant.

But his reference to that night reminded her sharply of how afraid she had been, of how she had been in terror until she realised just how capable she could be. The memory brought resentment with it.

"Did it occur to you that making fires and cooking was not necessary training for the daughter of a wealthy merchant?" She demanded angrily. "Did it enter your head that I might not survive?"

His eyes met hers and held her gaze for a few moments, making her wonder if he intended to reply. Finally he did, and it was not what she wanted to hear.

"If you want the honest truth," he replied thoughtfully, "no, it did not occur to me. At that precise moment, I really did not care whether you survived or not."

A lump formed in her throat, almost stopping her breath. Why did she have to ask these questions, when she knew the answer would only hurt?

"Later, though," he went on, "when I had calmed down, I made sure that you were watched, that you were managing."

"Anthony?" He nodded. "Is there anything he will not do for you?"

Richard shrugged as though it had never really occurred to him, while she realised he must have known about Charles Carlisle's visit. Why they were not both dead, she could not guess.

"You threatened to kill me if anyone discovered who I was and I am quite sure you meant it. I think you ask forgiveness for the wrong sin."

"Not at all," he replied quietly. "You were right, I did mean it. How I kept from strangling you with my bare hands, I will never know. But I could not have you running away and perhaps declaring your real identity. I needed you to believe me; it was essential for your safety and mine that you believed me. It was the only thing that would keep you from leaving the cottage, from showing yourself and giving yourself away."

"I might have stayed there simply because you asked me to."

"Once perhaps," he said, with a quizzical raise of his eyebrows. "Not any more. You are too headstrong. I was afraid you would want revenge."

She was not sure what any of that meant. Was he saying he had not meant it, that she had no need to fear for her life, that once he was calmer he regretted his threat? Or was he telling her he would have carried out his threat and still would, if the need arose?

It was all too confusing to her addled brain, especially now, with her little girl lost and nothing left worth going on for. Everywhere she looked there was a memory of her, of her first smile, her first steps, her first words – all her little achievements that her father had missed while he gave his time to two other women, the mad fanatic on the throne and the trollop in his bed.

She cast her eyes around the chamber she had not seen for so long, with the sunlight streaming through the windows, and compared it to the dark and tiny one roomed hovel with its wattle and daub walls, its mud floor. She had no doubt that Richard would now return her to that place, that this house for which she had paid so dearly was lost in her past and would never be hers again.

It was hopeless to think about it; she only wanted this day to be over and was almost looking forward to returning to her pauper's existence. At least there she would come to know her place, would not be forever hankering after the life she should have had. She wanted to leave, now, before she became too comfortable in this beautiful house.

"What now, My Lord?" She asked after a moment. "Am I to return to my peasant's life? I have become quite proficient at cooking and washing. I can even light a fire. I have not attempted to catch my own food as yet, but I expect I could do so if you insisted. You would be so proud of me." She watched him thoughtfully before she went on sarcastically. "It is cold in the cottage, though. I would be grateful for one of those fancy chimneys the rest of your tenants are enjoying."

He seemed to flinch at that and she wondered if he saw the irony of the tenants having chimneys, while his wife almost froze.

He got up and turned to the window, keeping his back to her.

"You will stay here, take up your place as my Countess. This will be a good enough reason for your substitute at court to leave, to retreat to the country in mourning. The Queen will not question it."

She wanted to know more, but she did not want more answers that would cause her pain. She had seen enough pain for one day. No doubt he had some other country house in which to keep his whore, perhaps closer to London, where he could visit often, where he could bed her without interference from his discarded wife.

"First I must send Robina back to France, back to the convent," he said. "She is a danger to you if she stays."

"So you heard her too."

He nodded. "She sees heresy in everything; I only let her stay because Anthony wanted it. I think even he is afraid to speak within her hearing. I was planning to get rid of her anyway."

Bethany stared at him, remembering how conveniently people had accidents in this place, but he gave her a little sardonic smile.

"Not what you are thinking," he said. "I will return her to France, tonight, before she has time to cause trouble. But you must promise me you will be quiet here. You must not put yourself in danger, not draw attention to yourself. It is nearly over."

"Over? What is over?"

"This reign. The Queen has had another imagined pregnancy. There is no Catholic heir to succeed her and that means the Scottish Queen or Elizabeth."

She watched him carefully, almost afraid to speak. To be talking of this was not safe and he knew it. Strange that one of the first things he talked about to her was the death of the monarch; it was no less dangerous now.

"What will that mean for you, My Lord," she asked. "You are Queen Mary's dearest friend and advisor. If she dies, Elizabeth will not spare you."

"Who knows what Elizabeth will do? I know nothing about her, only what the Queen has told me and her word is not to be trusted when it comes to her half sister." He turned back to her, looking at her thoughtfully as though he had more to say but was unsure of how much he should reveal. "Philip has returned to Spain, for good this time I think. The Queen is not well and her reaction to the loss of what she believes was another child and her husband, whom she fools herself into believing she loves, will likely send her over the edge. She has lost popularity since the execution of Cranmer and now she has lost Calais, our last territory in France."

"What does that mean exactly?"

"It means more burnings. It means more of the barbaric executions for which she will be remembered." His jaw was clenched, as were his fists, his voice rose angrily and she was surprised at this turn events had taken.

"I thought you approved. You said you did."

"And you believed me?" He asked with raised eyebrows.

"Why should I not believe you? You are Catholic, after all."

"And you are not, are you sweetheart, nor ever likely to be?" He ran his fingers through his hair in an agitated fashion then laughed that self deprecatory laugh. "Why did I think you ever would be? I wanted you because you were your own person, and then I thought I could make you follow me. What a fool I was."

He came towards her and held out his hand. She hesitated to take it; she was still hurt and angry and desperately unhappy about losing Alicia. She knew there would be no more children, for how could there be when they were no longer of one flesh? He might still want an heir enough to return to her bed, but it seemed unlikely. He appeared defeated somehow, as if it had all been for nothing.

Still he waited, his hand held out invitingly, until she finally took it. He pulled her to her feet and kissed her, but not with the passion of the past. This was just a goodbye kiss, a final gesture to mark the end of their life together.

"I must return to London tomorrow," he said. "The funeral will be in the morning and I will leave straight after. I will not see you again, but keep yourself safe please. The Queen is angry now. She believes God has deserted her because her efforts have not been vigorous enough. It would never occur to her it is because they are too vigorous. I can do little to curb her enthusiasm, neither can anyone else."

I will not see you again. She wondered what he meant by that but she could not bear to ask; she feared the answer too much.

She was about to follow him from the bedchamber when she heard Robina's voice in the gallery.

"Richard!" She cried. "What can I do for you? You have lost your only child and now you learn your wife is a heretic? How can you bear it?"

Bethany peered through the crack where the door opened to see Richard's furious expression.

"You talk nonsense, Robina," he replied angrily. "Bethany is as loyal to the church as you are."

"Then why did she try to stop Father Francis from giving that poor little girl her passage into Heaven? How can you say she is loyal when she could do that?"

"She has just lost her only child, Robina," he tried to reason with her. "She is a grieving mother and grieving mothers say and do all sorts of things they do not mean. You must understand that, or you have no right to call yourself a Christian."

She drew back a little at that, but went on regardless.

"I shall pray for her, Richard," she said. "And for you."

She turned and had started to walk away when he called after her.

"Robina, I think it best if you return to France, tonight if possible."

"What? Why? You will need me here, now more than ever."

"I am returning to court tomorrow, straight after the funeral. Why would I need you?"

She did not answer for a few seconds, then she finally spoke with determination and that same manic look in her eyes.

"Richard, I too am grieving for that little girl, but I do not try to send away God's messengers. Your wife needs my counsel, even if you do not."

Bethany thought he might strike her then, he looked so angry, and she suspected that anger was induced by fear. He knew what his wife would say to her counsel, she would not be able to help herself. Then they would all be in danger.

"You will return to France, tonight," he told her firmly. "I shall tell Anthony."

With that he turned and walked away, while Bethany could only hope she left before she destroyed them all.

***

She felt a sense of dread when he had gone. If Richard was right, and he usually was, there would soon be a protestant monarch on the throne once more. Bethany should have felt happy about that, but she was in the same position as five years ago when he went off to fight for Mary. He had torn her love apart, yet she still cared for him. She wanted him to be safe, even if she never saw him again, even if she had to give him up to his whore. She wondered briefly if she would ever be able to bring herself to speak her name.

It was strange, being back at Summerville Hall. Each morning for weeks she would open her eyes expecting to be on her little straw mattress in her dark little cottage and she always thought she was still asleep and dreaming. It was strange having the servants to do things for her again. It took a little while until she stopped trying to do them herself, as they thought it very odd when Her Ladyship tried to light the fire. She had no idea where her clothes were. The last time she had seen them, they were being taken away in the coach, but she need not have worried. Richard had, as always, thought of everything and they were carefully folded in the chest at the bottom of the bed.

Anthony was subdued around her, unable to converse in his normal relaxed manner. He knew what had happened, where she had been. He knew she had betrayed his cousin, something he could never forgive, so she expected nothing else.

"You do not have to speak to me, Anthony," she said. "The house is big enough I think so we need never meet."

He looked at her thoughtfully for a few moments then sighed heavily.

"If Richard can forgive you, it is not my place to do otherwise," he replied.

"Still letting Richard think for you, I see."

"Not at all," he replied stiffly. "It just happens that I disagree with him on this occasion, and that is not a position I am accustomed to."

"You think he should have left me where I was? You think he should not have forgiven me, allowed me back in this house?"

"I think he should have disposed of you when he had the chance, just like..." he stopped talking abruptly, as though he had said too much. "It is what I expected him to do."

She could only stare at him, totally shocked. Was this really Anthony talking? Gentle, considerate Anthony?

"Good thing for me, then, the decision was not yours." She was silent for a moment, wondering whether she really wanted an answer to her next question, but it had been tearing at her for months so she could not help but ask. "He did kill Rosemary, did he not?"

"I have always believed he did, yes, although I could not say for certain. It is not something he would ever discuss." He paused and stared at her, as though he was still wondering why Rosemary had to die, while Bethany, the real traitor, stayed alive.

"All I know is that he carried her body to London, to where my parents had just died of plague. He knew it was the best way to cover any foul play. What does that tell you?"

"If that is true, why do you suppose I escaped?"

He shrugged.

"Perhaps because you were the mother of his child," he said at last and the implication was clear. She was the mother of his child no longer.

She left him and went to walk around the grounds. Her steps took her unwillingly to the spot where the swing hung still and silent, to the forest from where she had spent so many hours watching her little girl play. Then she turned and walked deeper among the trees, where the little cottage still stood, silent and deserted.

She stood before the ill-fitting wooden door for some time, afraid to go inside lest some unseen force should lock her in, lest she could not find her way out again. She shook herself free of the irrational notion, then opened the door and took one step inside, leaving the door ajar so she could make an easy escape.

She did not think there was anything there she wanted until she caught sight of the little leather pouch that had been with her since the beginning. It was still attached to the belt of the peasant's dress she had been wearing when Richard arrived to reclaim her.

She wondered fleetingly if Belladonna kept its potency, as it would be useless if it did not. She picked it up and attached it to her waist. Who knows but she might still need it? Her husband might still decide to do away with her, when he realised she was of no further use to him.

For a little while she walked among the trees, easily recognising the one where he had first taken her as his wife. She could lie down there now and remember it, feel that thrill of first love once more, but why torment herself? It was over and done with and could never be retrieved.

CHAPTER TEN

There was little to do. She could ride out in the carriage and greet the villagers, who all believed she had been living in London all this time, she could ride out on horseback and be sure the tenants had enough supplies for the coming winter. At least she had someone to talk to, which came as a relief.

She was always greeted with joy by these people, as though merely by taking the time to visit she was conveying some great honour on them. She made sure they knew she was back in residence should they need anything. It was what the Earl would expect – at least she knew that much about him.

But they were all so eager to tell her how sad they were about losing little Lady Alicia. She could not bear it. Some of the women even came forward and hugged her as though she were a dear friend. She was rather touched by that, actually; it was how they had always greeted her husband, now it seemed she had been elevated to receive the same affection. Her father would have been horrified at the familiarity, but even more so that she was pleased by it.

She continued to walk about the grounds, even though there was now a chill in the air. The morning brought a mist with it, a dampness which would likely dry to sunshine later, but time was getting on and Christmas would soon be upon them again. Last Christmas she had spent alone, hidden beneath the fur covers to keep warm, and sobbed the day away. She wondered if Richard would return to Summerville and if he did, would he demand that his wife leave so he was not forced to spend time with her.

This year would soon be over, but still Mary reigned, still innocent people died.

Bethany was just about to leave the house that morning to go for her usual walk when Anthony stopped her. He had avoided speaking to her since her return, unless it was absolutely necessary. It made her sad, since she had become fond of him, but she could do nothing about it.

"It seems you have visitors," he said, glancing out of the window.

Seated on horseback was Sir Geoffrey Winterton, and in his hand he held the reins of another horse, upon which sat her brother's wife, Margaret. Bethany had not seen her or her brother since her marriage and she could not understand what she was doing, why she had gone to Geoffrey or why he had brought her here.

Bethany hurried outside.

"Sir Geoffrey," she greeted him.

"Take this woman off my hands, please," he demanded. "She came to me early this morning, looking for your sister. I am surprised she does not know how she betrayed me."

"Julia is dead, Sir," she replied. "Did you not know that?"

"I do now," he replied without so much as a flinch at the news. "That leaves me free to live as I wish. I have her money, which is all the good she ever was to me."

Bethany could not answer; she was too angry.

She stepped forward and took the reins of Margaret's horse, then led her toward the house as he rode away.

"Come inside, Margaret. Tell me what you are doing here."

But she just stared at her as though she had spoken another language. A groom arrived to take the horse, but still she sat in her saddle, making no move to dismount.

"Are you getting down?" Bethany asked her. "Are you going to come inside, have a drink and tell me where Michael is?"

"Michael? Michael is dead," she replied. "Along with his father and mother."

Bethany jumped at this news, then felt Anthony beside her, his hand on her arm. He stepped forward and took Margaret's feet out of the stirrups then lifted her to the ground. She thought she might resist, but she seemed in a trance.

"How?" She asked. "How did they die?"

"Murdered by the filthy Papists!" Margaret cried in a loud voice. Bethany looked at Anthony for a reaction, but he was calm as he handed her horse's reins to the groom.

"Take her inside," he said at last. "Before anybody hears her."

When she had refreshments and the servant had left them, Bethany took her hand and sat silently for a moment, wondering how best to question her. She was not the same, that was for sure. She had always been a quiet, shy little thing, with little to say for herself. She had hung off Michael's every word and agreed with everything he had to say; now she seemed to be slightly deranged.

"Tell me, Margaret," she began. "Why are you here? Is Michael really dead?"

Margaret turned and stared at her for a few moments, then put down her goblet and got to her feet.

"I do not want you!" She cried. "You are in league with the devil! I want Julia; where is Julia?"

"Julia is dead," Bethany answered. "Did you not hear me tell Sir Geoffrey that?"

"She has been murdered as well by the filthy idolaters? When will it end?"

"Margaret, you must keep your voice down. You speak heresy. You could get us all arrested."

"Heresy? In this house, the house of the arch idolater? Well now, would that not pollute these old walls?" She turned and looked around before she spoke again, while she prayed no servants were within earshot. "It will not be long now before he gets what he deserves. Loyal Protestants are working even now to put the Princess Elizabeth on the throne where she belongs."

"Margaret! You speak treason!"

"I will speak my mind!" She cried loudly. "Just as you have always done. You always shocked me with the way you spoke out, no matter what. Now I can see you were right, we should not spend our lives pretending just because we are women. Elizabeth will be Queen; Mary will die."

Anthony stood in the doorway, listening. His face was crimson with fury, his fists clenched at his sides.

"You are distraught, Margaret," Bethany said quickly. "I can see that. You need a good sleep. I will find you a bed and you can tell me what has happened later, when you wake."

She turned to Anthony with a plea in her eyes. He owed her no favours; he likely believed that every member of her family was determined to ruin his, but she needed his help now and she was not afraid to ask for it.

"Have we a sleeping draught?" She asked him. "She needs to sleep, then she will be able to see clearly. Then we can decide what is best to do."

He did not reply, only stared at her for a few minutes.

"I think I already know what to do, Bethany," he said quietly.

"She has lost her mind," she replied. "Can you not see that? She needs rest, then she will be better."

"Even a lunatic will speak only her true thoughts," he said, but he moved to his cupboard and came out with a bottle. "Give her this," he said handing it to her.

"What is it?" She asked as she removed the cork and sniffed.

"Poppy juice. Give her too much and she will not wake up; it is your choice."

She stared at him; was he seriously hinting that she should do just that?

While Margaret slept Bethany tried to decide what was best to do with her. She could not stay here, ranting about papists and plots to put Elizabeth on the throne. She would get them all killed. She ordered her taken to the east wing, that secret part of the house which was once more going to be put to use to protect a heretic. Another betrayal she would have to live with.

She took her supper on a tray, carefully locking the heavy door behind her.

"Margaret? Are you awake?"

She sat up and stared at Bethany, a look of contempt in her eyes like that she had seen in Julia's.

"You knew, did you not?" Margaret demanded. "You knew when you accepted his wealth that he was a filthy papist."

"That is all in the past now," Bethany replied. "Tell me what happened. My parents were going to France."

She shook her head violently.

"They never got there," she said. "*We* never got there. They were stopped, imprisoned." She took a bite of bread then glared at Bethany once more. "How did that happen, I wonder?" She demanded. "The evacuations were new then. Nobody knew about them, nobody but you."

"Me? You do not think I betrayed you, do you? My own parents, my own brother."

"Your mother said she wrote to you about it. How else did they find out?"

The letter. Mother's letter that Richard found, that he had returned to her. And she had believed him so generous to do so, while all the time he...she could not bear to think of it.

"But that was years ago," she went on. "How did you escape?"

"I got away when the soldiers came. I have had to work, Bethany. I have had to work in an inn to earn my keep like any low born woman. Because of him! Because of *your* husband."

She was not about to reveal how she had lived because of that same man. How Margaret would love to hear that!

"You do not know that it was Richard who betrayed you. If mother wrote to me, she could have told anybody. She was never any good at keeping a secret."

"It matters not who it was. He was the one who ordered it; he was the one who was in charge. Do not deceive yourself by thinking otherwise."

Bethany was beginning to realise that herself, that he was not the innocent bystander she tried to believe he was, but overlord of all this carnage.

"He will get what he deserves soon enough," Margaret was saying. "Elizabeth will be Queen and Lord Summerville and his cohorts will find themselves on the losing side at last. Now I am here you can help me."

She backed away, horrified.

"No! You must forget any plans in that direction. You are lucky Anthony has not already sent for soldiers."

"Him? He is no threat to me."

Bethany could see she was unbalanced or she would have seen the danger she was in, the danger she had put them all in. She got up and left the bedchamber, locking the door from the outside. She heard Margaret shout, jump to her feet.

"Bethany!" She screamed, hammering on the heavy door. "You cannot keep me locked up here. My friends will be here; I told them where I was going. Locking me up will not stop Elizabeth from becoming Queen!"

Nobody ever came near that part of the house, but there was always the risk they might.

"Well," Anthony's voice came from the bottom of the stairs. "What do you intend to do with her?"

She continued down the stairs to stand beside him. She could still hear Margaret hammering at the door, could still hear her screaming about her treacherous plans.

She made no reply, but moved to the settle where she sat down to think. She heard Anthony follow and enter the room behind her.

"What do you suppose I should do with her?" She asked him at last. "She is my brother's wife."

"She is a traitor. If she is not involved in a plot to murder Queen Mary, she deludes herself that she is. She is a danger to us all."

"But what can I do? I can keep her in the east wing, at least there she can do no harm."

"I can hear every word she is screaming, and so will everybody else. If you do not report her, then someone else will and it will look like we were hiding her, that we condoned her words. I will not risk a treason charge for some mad woman, even if she is your kin."

She studied him for a long time, wondering how the few years since they had met had left him so hard and cold.

"I cannot report her, for Michael's sake."

"Michael is dead. Get rid of her, Bethany, or I will."

She hoped Margaret would calm down, go back to sleep. She would take her more poppy juice, hope she would see reason, but when she went upstairs she could still hear her through the thick, oak doors to the east wing.

CHAPTER ELEVEN

"Margaret," Bethany pleaded. "If you promise to keep your voice down, to say nothing to anyone, I will help you."

It had been a week since she arrived and since then she had not left this chamber. Bethany had tried to reason with her, tried to convince her she was putting them all in danger, but she did not seem to understand. She ranted about Elizabeth, about how her friends would come, but there had been no sign of them as yet. Bethany did not believe that any serious conspirators would allow someone like Margaret to be included in their plans.

Margaret stared at her suspiciously, but she took her hands and sat beside her on the bed. Richard was right about one thing: pretence was not in her nature. This was going to be one of the hardest things she had ever had to do.

"Why would you do that?" She demanded. "You are the wife of the architect of it all, of the fanatic's greatest ally. You know, do you not, that once Elizabeth is Queen, your Lord will die as the traitor he is?"

Bethany swallowed hard, trying to put herself into another role, one in which she wanted Richard dead. It was the only way to convince her that she spoke the truth, but oh! It was almost unbearable to do.

"Do you imagine I enjoy seeing my friends die a horrible death? Do you imagine I am happy to be the wife of such a man? To have people believe I must agree with him, since he is my husband? He has humiliated me in the worst possible way." She wanted to say that his death would be a blessing, but she choked on the words. "I think Elizabeth should be Queen, just as you do. You must come with me to a place I know where it will be safe for us to meet, where you can bring your friends to plan properly without interference."

She still looked suspicious, but Bethany put her arm around her to comfort her fears.

"I watched Julia die," Bethany said, choking back tears. "I was there. You think I do not want an end to that? You think I do not want revenge for her death?"

She did not want to remember that, but she believed it was what swayed her in the end. Margaret hated Bethany's husband, as did her friends; it was easy enough for her to believe that his wife might also hate him.

"You be quiet here. You rest for now. Tonight, I will come for you and show you a place that is safe, a place that is secret. Will you do that for me?"

She nodded, then lie down on the pillow while Bethany slipped away, locking the door once more. Bethany would wait until after dark, until all the servants had gone to their beds, just as she had done before when leading those Protestants through the underground passage. That is where she intended to take Margaret, down beneath the house and into the crypt where she could slide the lid from the stone coffin of one of the Summerville ancestors and hide a body inside.

It would not be difficult to lure her there, she was sure. She had made her believe she was on her side easily enough, so why could she not have done the same to Mary Tudor? For the sake of the man she loved? But she was not desperate then, now she was.

She rested on her bed for a few hours, but real sleep evaded her. It was very dark when she emerged, carrying the leather purse and wrapped in her velvet cloak. She lit a candle to guide her through the dark passages of the house and at last arrived at the east wing. She took out the key to open the door to the bedchamber, but it was already unlocked. Had she forgotten to lock it? She was sure she had not; it was too important to their safety. She tiptoed and hoped the door made no noise, but there was no sign of anyone. Bethany searched through all the chambers; there was no sign of her. She could not have escaped, could she? Bethany cursed herself for being so gullible as to think she had convinced her sister-in-law where her own loyalties lay.

She went downstairs with the intention of looking outside, in case she was still in the grounds, but when she reached the door to the underground passage, she found it open. Margaret could not have found that door, it was well hidden, merged with the wall panelling.

The shuffling sound from the tunnel made Bethany step back, half expecting to see Margaret with that manic look in her eyes, but it was Anthony who emerged. His jacket was dishevelled, his shirt open and grubby and there was perspiration beading on his forehead.

"What have you done?" She asked.

"What you would not have done," he replied.

"But I…"

"Oh, I know what you had planned. I have been watching you, listening at doors. But you would never have done it and you would never have had the strength to lift the lid of one of those coffins."

Bethany stared at him, her eyes wide with shock.

"It had to be done, Bethany," he went on. "She was a danger to us all." He brushed his hands together to remove the grime and dust from the crypt. "It is done and nothing more to be said."

She watched him walk away, expecting to feel some sorrow for the passing of her brother's wife, but all she felt was relief. She could hardly be shocked at the sudden demise of the wife beater now, could she? At least he had deserved it. All Margaret had done was to lose her mind amid enough loss and terror to make a saint go mad.

Some future generation of curious descendants might open that stone sarcophagus, and they would wonder why one of those boxes contained the bones of two people. Perhaps they would think them lovers, buried together, but they would never know for sure. Nobody would know except Bethany and Anthony that the bones were those of her only brother's widow, come to her for help.

She rose early the following morning to walk in the grounds and clear her head. Autumn was upon them, there was a damp chill in the air and Bethany pulled her cloak closely about her, clutching the two sides together to keep out the cold and feeling the blame for what had happened to Margaret.

She walked as far as the trees before she stopped, not wanting to get close to the priest's cottage, still afraid it might reach out and grab her. She turned back toward the house to see what looked like a messenger leaving the house. They did not get so many of those, not since Anthony now knew how to run things without Richard's constant instructions, so she was naturally curious.

When she approached the house she saw that Anthony wore a worried frown and his face clearly showed his distress. In his hand he held a piece of unrolled parchment, bearing very familiar handwriting.

"I have bad news," he said. "Come inside, please."

They went into the smaller room which was more comfortable for sitting than the great hall. The fire was alight and glowing, making it warm, and Anthony sat opposite to her. She wondered what he had to tell her. After all, bad news to him might well be good news to her, but that was Richard's handwriting. She would recognise it anywhere and she wondered what sort of bad news he had to impart, at least of the type that she could be warned about.

"Well?" She prompted.

"I have just received this despatch from London," he said gravely. "It is from Richard. He is in the Tower."

"What?" She jumped to her feet and grabbed the letter from his fingers. "Why? I do not understand."

"Read it. It seems he is convicted of treason."

Her legs dissolved beneath her and she collapsed onto the settle behind her. She could do nothing but stare at the familiar writing, though not a single word she read made any sense.

"So the Queen has discovered she has been lied to?" She whispered hoarsely.

"I imagine that is the reason. I can think of no other, unless of course she has learned of your own deceptions."

She hardly knew how to answer and she sat staring at him for a long time, hoping he would see the folly of his words.

"No, Anthony!" She cried out, finally finding her voice. "You will not blame me for this! Do you see any guards come to arrest me?"

He shook his head slowly.

"Forgive me," he said at last. "I am distraught." He took the letter and waved it at her. "Did you read this? He has been convicted already not just charged. I knew nothing about a trial. He goes to the block tomorrow."

His words tore through her like a sword and while she tried to stand, all her strength seemed to have drained away. Her anger with Richard, the resentment she had carefully nurtured since he banished her to the life of a peasant, dissipated in a second. She would never see him again, she really would never see him again. The forgiveness she so wanted from him could never now be sought, the love she still had for him could never now be spoken of.

"I have to go to him," she said at last. "I have to see him."

"They will not let you in," Anthony replied.

"Why not? I am his wife."

"And he will not want you to announce that, you must understand." Anthony started pacing the floor urgently. "If he is a traitor then you could be condemned as well."

"I do not think I care very much," she said after some thought. "What have I got to lose? My child has gone, my husband has gone. I have nothing else."

"Richard has written that neither of us is to go to London lest we be arrested, too." He paused then turned away as he went on. "It is best to do what he wants."

"And I have had enough of what Richard wants," she replied firmly. "Richard wanted to spend his time with that woman. He wanted me to stay and live like a peasant, so that no one would know. I did everything he wanted, because he wanted it. No more. Now I must do what I want, and I want to see him." She turned to look at him thoughtfully, a doubt coming into her mind. "But you must stay here," she said. "What will happen to Summerville if you are arrested?"

"There will be no Summerville, Bethany. If Richard is executed as a traitor, all his wealth and his property will be forfeit to the crown. You and I will have nothing."

"Then there is really no reason to stay, is there? I am to lose my home and my title because he could not keep his hands off his trollop, but still I am going to London. Still I have to see him one more time. Who is the fool now? You must be very satisfied to see me brought to this." He made no reply, but she thought she saw his expression turn to one of dismay. "Are you coming with me?"

***

Richard had given his last few coins to the gaoler in exchange for writing materials. He was not sure how much would be left, if Summerville and all its lands and properties would be forfeit, but he wanted to make a Will. He had valuable jewels he wanted Bethany to have, even if she sold them. She might have to and even if she was not forced to it through need, he would not blame her.

He sat on the ledge beside the window where there was just enough light to see by and looked around at the cold, stone cell, at the straw covered floor. He pulled his fur cloak tightly about his shoulders and closed his eyes.

It would soon be over. Rachel was safe, at least, and if Bethany no longer loved him, as he believed, she would be free to marry again if that was her wish. The thought of her with another man twisted his heart, but he knew he deserved it. He had allowed her to love him, then he had thrown her love back in her face by letting her think he loved someone else.

He had imprisoned her in that freezing cottage to live like a peasant for a year, he had separated her from her only child, and he had viciously attacked her. Of course she no longer loved him. He had killed that love.

What a damned fool he was! Tomorrow he would go to his death, a public execution on Tower Hill. He would lay his head down on a wooden block, already stained with the blood of long dead traitors, before a jeering crowd and he would begin his journey through purgatory. He expected that journey to be a long one for he had many sins for which to atone.

But none of it mattered. He had lost everything in this life he ever loved; he had lost Summerville, he had lost Bethany and his daughter, and he had put Rachel's safety at risk. He looked forward to the dawn, when it would all be over.

He had written to Anthony, telling him what had happened, and now his will was almost finished. He had written a letter to Rachel, too, but he had no idea how he would get it to her. No one must suspect that she was the woman who had impersonated the Countess of Summerville and insulted the Queen by taking Bethany's position as her lady in waiting. He would roll the letter up and put it beneath his collar, that way his blood would obliterate it if he could find no other way to get it to her.

There was but one wish he would want granted and that would be to hold Bethany in his arms once more, to kiss her lips and feel her heart beating against his, to make her believe he loved her even if she no longer loved him.

He thought it was a hopeless wish, until the key turned, the door opened and he looked up from his writing to see his wish standing before him.

***

Anthony nodded then took his cloak down from the board and ordered the horses saddled.

They rode for some hours to get to London, stopping to change horses at an inn in Cambridge. There was a feeling of urgency about the journey, even though they both knew there was still time and there was nothing either of them could do to save him. She was in a panic the whole way there lest something happened to delay them, lest they should arrive too late or not be allowed access.

There was a mist hanging over the distant grey buildings, as though it had come in his honour, had come to aid him on his journey to the hereafter. They drew rein and sat on their horses and watched the old building, imagining the horrors that had gone on there. Bethany wondered behind which little window he was, she wondered if he could see daylight.

They dismounted, left their horses at the stable while they took the boat down the river to the entry gates. They passed traitor's gate, the one Richard would have been taken through, the one the Princess Elizabeth is said to have refused to enter. They say she sat down on the steps and would not move, declaring that she was no traitor.

As they passed beneath London Bridge, she shivered with horror when she saw the heads, some rotting and putrid, some fresh and still wet with blood. She recalled the words she spoke to Richard at one of their earliest meetings, that she would hate to see his head up there on the bridge. It would be there though, would it not? Come tomorrow, his handsome head would be up there on a spike with all the other traitors. It was a ghastly sight, made even worse by knowing there would be one more tomorrow.

They had both got out of the boat at the quayside, but she wanted to go in alone. What she had to say to Richard was for him alone.

"Well," Anthony said. "Are we going, or have we come all this way for nothing?"

"I will go first," she said. "If you do not mind."

"You are welcome, My Lady. But I would advise against revealing your true identity."

She nodded and began to climb the slippery, stone steps. Inside, it was dark and damp, and there was water running down the walls. It was little wonder prisoners of this place died of lung rot after many years of incarceration. At least Richard would be spared that.

It was not as hard to get in as she had imagined. It seemed gold coin was as effective here as anywhere else. Nobody searched her, nobody enquired as to her identity, not until she got to the actual cell door, then it seemed Anthony's warnings were in vain.

"So you are the real wife, then," the guard said brusquely. "The genuine article. I would give a lot to know what the man has, that you would still willingly make this journey, enter this terrible place, just to see him, after all he has done to you." Bethany gazed at him, astonished by his words. How did he know who she was? Then he went on. "Or have you come to gloat?" He said. "Have you come to see him brought down? Nobody would blame you."

She shook her head.

"No. I would never do that. Yes, I am his real wife and I am proud to be so. Are you going to allow me to see him?"

The guard nodded. She thought about how it must have looked to him. This wealthy, titled man had kept his mistress at court, risked his life in so doing, while his lawful wife languished in the country. Yet she still wanted to see him, to say goodbye to him, even though he was here for the sake of that other woman, not her.

The guard turned the key and pushed the door open. It was dark inside and took a few moments to accustom her eyes; she blinked to focus and she saw Richard. He sat on a stone ledge beneath the window, writing with a quill and parchment. His fine silk shirt was grubby and there was blood drying on the sleeve. She wondered only fleetingly if it were his blood or someone else's. It hardly mattered after all. Over the shirt he wore a cloak of fur, which he would need in this place. The stone floor was strewn with straw and there were no other furnishings so she suspected the straw covered floor was where he slept.

Scuffling in the corner as the light came in from the open door made her step back in alarm. Rats, startled by the sudden light scampered away into the darkness.

There was a little light coming from outside, enough to see him raise his head and look up. He laid down the writing materials and stood quickly, then he took a step forward as the guard left and closed and locked the door behind him. The sound of the key turning sent a chill along her spine.

She had heard many horror stories about this place and her first impression was that they were all true. She could imagine nothing worse than being locked in here, with the damp and the cold and the rats, without even the small comfort of a mattress or a cover with which to warm herself. She desperately wanted to turn and run, but she also wanted to take him in her arms and comfort him. She chose the latter option; if this was her last chance to see Richard, then she must take it, no matter how gruesome the surroundings.

She had come this far, still uncertain of her welcome. It could be that he had no wish to ever see her again; she would not blame him.

"Bethany? Is that really you?" He asked softly.

Her carefully prepared self control collapsed and she ran to him, no longer caring whether he wanted her or not. The last few years melted away. What did it matter that he had hurt her? What difference that he had chosen his whore over her and that she had lived those years in fear of him? She was about to lose him forever and this time was all that mattered now. *Just do not let him tell me I am not welcome,* she pleaded silently. She thought she could have borne anything but that.

She felt his arms wrapping around her, holding her close, something she had missed so much, and she slipped her hand inside his shirt and ran her fingers over his nipple. She kissed his chest where his shirt fell open.

She felt hard metal on her cheek and moved her head back to look at the large oval locket which hung from a chain between his breasts. She had never seen that before and now she took a deep breath to gather enough courage to open it, expecting to see the perfect face of the beautiful Rachel staring back at her.

He made no move to stop her as her fingers found the clasp and she gasped to see her own face, a tiny version of the face in the painting which hung in his bedchamber at Summerville Hall. What on earth did that mean? She would not ask, but she realised now how the guard had recognised her. He must have seen this locket.

"You should not be here," Richard whispered urgently. "It is too dangerous."

"I care nothing for danger. I had to see you."

He pulled her into his arms and kissed her, a real kiss, not like the last one they had shared, a kiss that aroused those feelings which were half forgotten, which she had tried so hard to forget. He pulled off her headdress and cast it onto the floor amid the straw, then unfastened her hair and ran his fingers through it, holding her head gently to look up at his face. He looked drawn and haggard, but was still the most handsome man she had ever seen.

"Oh, my love," he whispered with a note of remorse. "I did not want you to see me like this."

"How, Richard?" She demanded. "How did you come to this?"

"Convicted of high treason you mean? Me, the Queen's most devoted and loyal servant? It is ironic, is it not?"

"I cannot believe you fell this far for a woman, you of all people. I hope she was worth it?"

His eyes swept over her and there was a gentle little smile playing around his lips as he spoke.

"Oh yes," he said. "She was definitely worth it."

A sob caught in her throat and tears sprang to her eyes, blurring her vision. So that wretched woman, that whore was to invade their last moments together. He would go to his grave still loving her, still wanting her and not even remembering how much his wife loved him.

"These will be our last moments together," she mumbled through her tears, "yet still you find words to hurt me. God in heaven, do you really hate me that much?"

He laughed then, that self deprecatory laugh.

"If I could hate you this would all have been easy," he said, keeping his voice low, then he pulled her close. "You do not think I was speaking of Rachel, do you? Would that I had time to tell you all about her, but time is something I have little of. I installed her as my wife to keep attention away from you, to keep you safe. She has been well compensated for her services."

She could scarcely believe what she was hearing. He had raped her, threatened to kill her and left her to live as a peasant in that freezing cottage, and now he was saying he was in this filthy cell for her sake? She did not believe him; he was saying these things to make her feel better, to make himself feel better.

"Just how far did those services go, My Lord?"

"I refuse to answer that. I shall never see you again. I will not waste the time talking about her and besides, I do not want us to be overheard. Nobody knows the name of the lady in question, and I would like to keep it that way." He turned to the letters he had been writing, then handed them to her. "It is only my Will," he said, "and a letter to Anthony. I dare write nothing more, though there is so much more to say."

"Anthony is outside," she told him. "He too wants to see you, to say goodbye."

He shook his head vehemently. "No. He cannot come here. It is too dangerous. I will not see him. There is so much I want to tell you, to explain, but if they let you in they must intend to listen. That is my only regret now, that you will never understand." He pulled her to him once more and his voice was low when he spoke. "Just know this: I have loved you more than life itself." Then he kissed her lips and slipped his hand inside her bodice to caress her breast. "You must go now, please. I fear for your safety if you stay."

I have loved you more than life itself. That is what he had said, but how could those words be true?

Was he just giving her something to remember, something to live on when he was gone?

"When will they..?" She began but she could not finish.

"Cut off my head?" He replied. "At dawn tomorrow."

He was so calm, so brave, as though his awful fate was of no importance, as though his appointment with the executioner was just like any other, like any day.

She had a vision of him laying his beautiful head down on that block, of some incompetent axe man hacking it off as they had that of Margaret Pole. It was rumoured she was cut to shreds about the neck and shoulders before her head finally left her body, before she finally died.

Bethany imagined the unruly crowd cheering at the death of a traitor, as they always did whether they believed him guilty or not. She could not bear it; the humiliation of this proud man who was her husband would haunt her for the rest of her life.

Then she remembered the little leather pouch which still hung at her waist.

"Wait, Richard," she said, without thinking. "I have this." She unhooked the pouch and opened it so he could see the contents. "There is no need for the public humiliation."

"Poison?" He asked with a puzzled frown. "Suicide?"

He was shaking his head slowly

"What is wrong? Have I angered you again?"

He closed her fingers over the leather pouch.

"You are not thinking, are you? Would you have my soul burn in hell for all eternity?"

No, she had not been thinking. Suicide was a mortal sin, the greatest of all.

"Forgive me," she whispered.

"No matter." Then he kissed her one last time and pushed her toward the door. "Now go, please."

Anthony was still waiting, seated on the damp stone wall outside.

"He will not see you," she told him as she took the hand of the boatman to help her into the waiting craft, leaving him to follow. Nothing was said as they collected their horses and began the long journey home, a journey she did not want to make. She wanted to stay there and hold her husband in her arms till the very last second of his life, but that would not be permitted either by the guards or by him.

They rode on in silence for some time, reaching the gates of the city before Anthony spoke.

"How does he look?"

She stared at him, thinking what a stupid question that was.

"He looks like a man about to meet his maker," she replied. "How did you expect him to look? Better? Like he might recover?"

She was angry, angry with him and angry with herself for wasting so much precious time. Would it really have been that hard to pretend, for his sake?

"You were wrong, you know," she told him.

"Wrong? About what?"

"He never hated me. He never wanted me dead. He loves me; he told me so just now, for the very first time ever, and the last. I shall live on those words for the rest of my miserable life." *Just as he intended,* she thought.

She rode away then, leaving him to stare after her.

CHAPTER TWELVE

Bethany stayed up that night, afraid to sleep. She kept the fire going and walked about the room just picking things up and studying them, as though she would never see them again. She did not want the dawn to come. She felt that if she did not sleep, she could hold back time like King Canute trying to hold back the waves. She did not want to waste this night, this last night, for it is hard to part with today when you know you must face tomorrow.

The dawn found her dozing, despite her efforts. She awoke with a start, thinking she had just had the worst nightmare ever, then she realised it was no nightmare after all, it was real. This morning she would be a widow, this morning she would say goodbye forever to the only man she could ever love. And Richard would go down in the history books as a traitor to his Queen.

She fought off sleep during that long night, wondering what she could do to make things even a little better. She thought about suicide, thought seriously, and the only thing that stopped her was Richard's reaction when she had suggested it to him. *Would you have my soul burn in hell for all eternity?* That is what he had said, and he had meant it. He would prefer to face the executioner, prefer to brave the humiliation of the cheering spectators, those 'guests' who would be privileged to have an invitation to the beheading of an Earl. He would rather face all that than risk his soul by taking his own life, in private, with dignity. And if he was right, if there was no paradise for a suicide, then Bethany would have thrown away any chance she might have had to meet him again. It was not worth the risk, but that did not stop her from thinking about it.

And what was she going to do with the rest of her life? It was the custom for the monarch to find a new husband for a countess and she wondered if that still applied when she would probably lose her title as well as her home. The Queen might think she had suffered enough, to be cast aside while her husband kept his mistress close beside him. Or she may be angry enough to decide it was her fault, that had she been a good wife he would not have looked elsewhere.

If she had to choose it would be the latter. She had lived as a peasant before, she could do it again; anything was better than a forced marriage to someone else. No one could ever replace Richard, no one could ever hold her in his arms and make her feel what she had felt for him, what she always would feel for him. The idea of another man in her bed, in his place, touching her, made her shudder and look more closely at the little leather pouch. Should it come to that, she still had the option to take the veil, though that would be hypocrisy at its worst.

One thing she had to do before she made that final decision was to ride out and tell the tenants their lord was no more, that his lands would be forfeit and given to someone else and whoever that someone else might be, it was certain he would not be building chimneys and making sure they had enough to eat.

She was uncertain about her ability to do that, but it was what he would have wanted, what he would expect of his countess.

She met Anthony in the great hall, where he had just finished announcing their fate to the servants.

"I will go now," she told him. "It is my place to inform the tenants."

"As you wish."

She watched him for a few moments, wondering what was going on in his mind. He must be heartbroken too; had he considered his own future? He seemed to be struggling to hold himself together, just waiting for a private moment when he could submit to the pain he must be feeling.

"And what about our fate, Anthony?" She asked with hesitation. "Yours and mine."

Bethany had no idea if he had property of his own, if he had even thought about what would become of her. Her family was gone, her father had disowned her in his Will. She had nothing now, nothing that Anthony did not choose to give her.

She thought of Charles Carlisle as a last resort. He would protect her for Julia's sake and if she had to live with her son, with Richard's son, there were worse things. At least the child would remind her of his father, as if she would ever need reminding.

"I have a house my father left me," Anthony said quietly. "You may come and live there with me, if you wish."

"Thank you. It is good of you."

"It is for Richard's memory that I make the offer, make no mistake about that. Were it left to me, you could go back to the cottage in the woods, or starve on the streets for all I care." His voice rose angrily as he spoke and she could only stare at him, stunned. So, he too, really hated her. "It is your fault he is dead, and for that I cannot forgive you, not even for Richard's sake."

"How is it my fault? I did not tell him to present another woman as his wife."

"He wanted a wife who could stand beside him, who would honour him. You could not do that for him, could you? So he had to find a substitute and for that he has died, executed as a traitor." His eyes held hers for some moments before he added: "No, for that I can never forgive you."

She turned away and wiped away tears with her sleeve. She badly needed comfort; she had hoped Anthony and she might mourn together, find comfort in each other's grief, but that would never happen now.

Was he right? Was it her fault Richard was dead? As she rode toward the cottages she tried to recall his words to her when she last saw him, that he had done what he had for her. She had not believed him, but perhaps Anthony was right, perhaps he was trying to protect her. *I have loved you more than life itself.*

There were many people gathered outside the cottages when she rode up, men as well as women. It was unusual for the men to be about during the day, even at this early hour, and she could only guess that they already knew what had happened, that they were here to learn what the future might hold for them.

"My Lady!" A woman cried, causing the crowd to break apart and come forward. She dismounted, let them take her hands, even hug her. They already knew the news, of course. She should have known. Most of the women were weeping and the ones who were not were obviously holding back their tears.

But Bethany could not cry. To cry would be to accept his death and she was not yet ready for that.

"My Lady, what will become of us all?" One man asked. "It is so wrong. His Lordship was such a good man; he did not deserve the death of a traitor."

As he spoke his voice rose and a woman came and tugged at his arm.

"Have a care, Will," she said urgently. "You should have a care what you say."

It was Connie, the woman whose late husband had abused her. Bethany remembered now her asking permission to remarry. She remembered Richard insisting on meeting the man, to assure himself she was not about to make another disastrous mistake.

"And who here is going to turn me in?" Will replied hotly. "Who here does not agree with me?"

"Connie is right, Will," Bethany said quickly. "It is always harder to hold one's tongue, but it needs to be done. Had I been able to hold mine, none of this would have happened. His Lordship would not want you putting yourself in danger for his sake." She looked about at the anxious faces; what could she do to help them? Nothing, it seemed. "I have no knowledge," she began, "of what the future holds. I wish I could assure you all, but I do not even know what my own future may hold."

There was a babble of voices at that, and through the confusion she heard that she would always have a roof over her head, poor though it would be. She was touched, and began to consider that sharing with one of these good people might be a preferable option to the offer which Anthony had so grudgingly made.

You want to feel you have been chosen, not tolerated. They were Richard's words when he proposed marriage and they were as true now as they had been then. Would this be an end to her story? That she would live out her days as the live in, mysterious relative of one of these good people? What would their new lord have to say about that?

It was all so heartbreaking, she could barely keep from crying, but each time she thought of a new path, the only one which appealed was inside that little leather pouch.

She had almost made up her mind while she fought off sleep during the long night, but now she was sure. She did not know whether the church was right or not, and somehow she did not care, but there were some duties she had to carry out before she could put an end to her misery.

Her first stop was the parish church in the village. In all the time she had been Countess of Summerville, she had never willingly set foot inside a Catholic church, always it had been to keep up appearances, to make people believe she was a good Catholic, and each time had been with a sense of deep dread. But her journey now was the most important of all, not to her, but to her husband.

She had no idea what to expect of the priest, whether he sympathised and mourned like the tenants in the cottages, or whether he rejoiced in the death of a traitor. She did know, however, that this whole village, including his church, belonged to Summerville and until such time as the family was replaced, he owed his very life to them.

"My Lady!" He said, coming forward immediately. "I am so glad you came to me for comfort. His Lordship was much loved; all the village is grieving."

"Thank you, Father," she replied, somewhat reassured. "I have not come for comfort for myself but to request masses be said for His Lordship's soul." She pulled off the diamond ring which she wore and handed it to him. Her memory showed her the day Richard had given it to her, when she had given birth to Alicia; *a gift for the mother of my child.* And even when she had been so desperate, she could not bear to part with it. Now she would give it up willingly, just to prove to Richard, wherever he was, that she could follow his wishes, albeit too late. "This is all I have, Father. Will it be enough?"

He stared at the ring in her hand for a few seconds then closed her hand over it, shaking his head.

"No, My Lady. You keep that. His Lordship will have all the masses I can give him. He was a good man, a kind and considerate man. I am quite sure God will spare him time in purgatory."

She thanked him and left, afraid those tears she was keeping locked up would burst out and start to fall.

It was almost noon when she got back to the house. She had been a widow now for four or five hours; she thought she would feel something when they did it, that she might feel the pain as well, but there was nothing. She could tell herself he was still at court, still helping Mary with her persecutions, still lying to his Queen; still taking his whore to his bed. She stood and stared at his portrait in the gallery, his handsome face, his playful smile. The clever artist had even captured his dancing black eyes and the muscles in his arms and she could almost feel them around her, hugging her close and arousing passion in her.

It was easy to tell herself he would soon be back, doing just that. She could tell herself all those things, she could look to the door each time she heard a sound, expecting him to be there, but she could not believe. Not when she knew different, not when she knew that very soon she would have to leave this place she had paid such a high price for, leave with Anthony, to be tolerated not chosen.

He was sitting beside the fire when she went in, just staring at the flames as though he could see something important within the dancing colours. There were tears in his eyes and she knew by the redness around them that he had hurriedly dried those tears when he heard her coming. He looked up at her with the same hatred she had felt earlier and she could tell he still believed her to be entirely to blame for Richard's death. Perhaps he was right, but she did not want to accept it. She wondered how soon he would begin to call himself Earl of Summerville. Would he still be able to claim the title, or would that be confiscated as well as the estate? Not that it mattered; without Richard, nothing mattered.

"Do we have any money?" She asked abruptly. "When Summerville is gone, what will be left?" He only stared at her with a scowl. "That Will Richard was writing, did it include provision to say masses for his soul?"

"It did. Why do you ask?"

"I only want to be sure. I have been to the church in the village to ask for masses, but the priest there would not take my ring in payment. I wanted to be sure."

"Why? You do not believe he needs them, do you?"

"No, but he did. It gives me some comfort to know he will have his masses, even though he has no need of them. It is all I can give him now."

His expression softened a little, making her feel that at least she had done one thing right in his eyes.

"I have heard nothing about what will happen," he said. "I think we need to gather our belongings together, so that we are ready when the time comes."

He got to his feet then and left the room, went upstairs to begin supervising the packing of his things, while she sat and stared at those flames, looking for some answer to her question. What did the future hold now?

***

She took the little leather pouch from her waist and tipped the battered berries into her hand. They left a stain on her skin that might give her away but she cared nothing for that. So what if they buried her at the crossroads, or outside the churchyard? It meant nothing to her, it never had.

It was beginning to be very tempting, despite what Richard believed. She was unsure about the Protestant church's beliefs on suicide, but she thought they were similar. There was no paradise for someone who recklessly threw away the precious gift of life God gave them.

Was there anything left to do, anything Richard would want from her? She had said her piece to the tenants, for all the good it did. She had arranged for her husband's soul to be looked after in accordance with his own beliefs. What about her soul? Should she be arranging her own funeral, or would she be denied such a thing should she take the course she was considering?

Was there anything left for which to stay? She contemplated her future, bereft of all she held dear and living under the protection of a man who despised her, who would happily see her dead were it not for his love and respect for her late husband.

She thought about the girl she once was, that Christmas of 1552 when the world was a safe and steady place, when she felt secure in the knowledge that England had a Protestant king and a Protestant heir to follow him, when there were no Catholics left free in England and when her only concern was how to escape a marriage to a poverty stricken minor baron, when an offer to trade her beliefs for wealth and power had meant nothing more than words.

She had read Belladonna to be a poison which caused no pain, but it did cause hallucinations and she wondered what she would see, whether they would be good hallucinations. Perhaps she would believe Richard was there, come to take her soul to paradise. She might even hold her little Alicia in her arms once more; that idea was tempting in itself, even if it were only a delusion.

She made up her mind at last, although she was very frightened. She tilted her hand and held it up to her face, sniffed the berries, just to get an idea of how they might taste, when she felt a strong grip on her wrist, forcing her to tip the berries out on to the floor.

"Do not try to stop me, Anthony, please," she pleaded. "There is nothing left for me now."

The voice which replied was one she never thought to hear again.

CHAPTER THIRTEEN

"It would seem I arrived just in time."

She spun around, her heart leaping. Had she taken some of the berries after all, without realising? There could be no other explanation for the vision which stood before her now, or perhaps she had indeed lost her mind.

"Richard?" She took his face between her hands, just to be sure he did not disappear, that he was not part of her night's dreams. "What are you doing here? Did the Queen change her mind?"

"Mary is dead," he said shaking his head. "Elizabeth has pardoned all her sister's enemies."

She held him tightly against her, so afraid he was indeed an hallucination which would vanish if she did not hold on tight.

"What were you thinking?" He said. "Suicide? Do you realise what that means?"

"It means I would not be buried in consecrated ground, nothing more. Would you have me believe that heaven lies beneath the ground within the churchyard walls, while hell yawns beneath the ground outside them?"

He kissed her then, his lips warm and hungry on hers. God! She had missed that!

"Had I got here and found you dead," he said, "I might have been tempted to take the rest myself."

He pulled her into his arms and she felt his heart hammering loudly against her face as he held her tightly.

At last they sat together and he put his arm around her while she rested her head on his chest. His warmth ran through her, wiping out all the bad memories of the past few years. She still did not understand how he had allowed himself to almost end his life on the block, this man who was always in control, always knew exactly what he wanted and how to get it. None of it mattered now; all that mattered was that she was in his arms, where she never thought to be again, and she held on tight lest he slip away.

But had he only come to tell her he was free? She'd not forgotten what she had done to him, she had not forgotten that she had not yet asked forgiveness. She did not want to ask the question, but she had to know if she was building false hopes.

"Will you be staying, My Lord?" She asked at last.

"If you will have me," he replied.

"Can you doubt it?" She replied. "I love you, Richard. You must know that, but what of her? Am I supposed to forget that you risked everything to be near her?"

"Never for her, my love. It was all for you." He paused long enough to kiss her, then went on. "But that was only part of it. Mary might have forgiven me for that, but not for aiding Protestants to escape to France."

She could almost find the irony in that. The arch papist is what Charles' followers called him, hardly someone likely to be guilty of that. It was that other charge which concerned Bethany.

"If you did not love Rachel, why did you present her at court as your wife? Why risk so much for a woman you say meant nothing to you?"

"It was never for her. I told you, it was for you."

"How? How could all this heartache possibly have been for me?"

"After that first time in the Queen's presence, I knew you would not be safe at court. Yet Mary wanted you for a lady in waiting. I could not refuse her, could I? I had to give her someone." She felt his gaze on her, as though he was thinking about the best way to tell her more. "The first time I took Rachel to court, I was sure someone would know, if not the Queen herself then someone. It only needed for one of my enemies to have taken more notice of my wife the first time she was there, but it seems you did not make much of an impression. Thank God."

"Did she know how dangerous it was? Why would she risk so much?"

"Do not imagine she was in love with me. I have known Rachel for many years; she loves me, yes, but it was never an intimate, romantic love. She is a dear friend, nothing more."

Bethany did not want to argue, to spoil this moment, but it hurt for him to confirm that this woman loved him. Did he also love her in return?

"So you did it to keep me safe, to keep attention away from me?" It was all she could do to keep from bursting into tears, she felt so ashamed. "And I used the privilege to betray you. Can you ever forgive me?"

"There is nothing to forgive. I realised that a long time ago."

"You hated me; I know it. When did you stop hating me, when did you start wearing my image next to your heart?"

"I did hate you, yes. When I came to fetch you, so you could say goodbye to our daughter, I had no intention of releasing you. I intended to take you back to the priest's cottage when it was over. I might have found you somewhere more comfortable to live once the Queen died, but that day I had no wish to face you. Yet you had a right to be with your child in her last moments and I would never have lived with my conscience had I denied you that right. I expected a meeting of two people who despised each other."

She caught back a sob.

"So you despised me?"

"Yes, until I saw you. You looked awful, so thin and pale, I just wanted to fold you up in my arms and make you better. I realised what I had done, how I had thrown everything away. When I left here after we buried our little girl, I no longer hated you; I realised how much I still loved you."

She kissed his lips, then wrapped her arms tighter around him. She was silent for a few moments as she tried to collect her scattered thoughts. So what was Rachel to him? And did it matter? She thought of the other charge of which he said he was convicted but it made no sense. Could it be the Queen had found out about her own betrayal and he had taken the blame upon himself? She would never live with that.

"Why should the Queen believe you had been helping Protestants to escape? I can imagine no one less likely to be guilty of that."

"Who do you imagine has been sending warnings to Charles Carlisle?"

"You?" She sat up, astonished. "Why would you do that? He hates you, more than anyone on earth."

"I know."

"Then why?"

He took a deep breath and drew her closer to him; it was a few minutes before he replied.

"If Carlisle were arrested, who would care for my son?" He replied.

She pulled away to look into his eyes.

"You knew about the boy? Julia was so careful to keep it from you. How did you find out?"

"I was watching Carlisle and his followers, waiting for an opportunity to arrest the lot of them, and I saw the child. I suspected straight away, but then your sister emerged from the house. I did try to save her, Bethany, I promise you that."

She believed him. He had no reason to lie.

"The child?" She prompted him. "Simon."

"Is that his name? Well I knew at once he was mine. So there I was, supposed to be hunting down the most wanted of all the heretics, and instead I found myself having to protect him. How ironic was that?" He paused and looked up at the ceiling reflectively. "How would he feel when he grows up, I thought, knowing his father had been the destruction of the only man he knew as a father? I could not do it, Bethany, I simply could not do it. And I had come to disagree with the Queen's policies by then anyway. It was no real hardship to betray her."

"But Charles has to be told," I said. "He thinks..."

"I don't care what he thinks. It is over now and I'll not talk about him any more."

She had no wish to spoil this moment, but there was more to say, whether he liked it or not.

"So you condemned me to that freezing hovel for helping the Protestants, while you were risking everything to do the same? I had no idea you were a hypocrite."

He stiffened, but it had to be said.

"It is true," he said. "I was sending warnings, but with little danger to myself. You were not privy to that. As far as you knew I was firmly on the side of the Queen and her campaign. I was angry because you were using everything I held dear to betray me, my house, my land, my church. Had you been discovered by anyone else, I would have lost everything. That's what made me so angry." He drew a deep breath to control his rising resentment at the memory. "Whether I was justified or not, I do not know. I only know I was too enraged to think logically or fairly. I wanted to punish you; I almost killed you."

She could see he was still angry about it, and she could hardly blame him.

"And my parents?" She asked. "My brother?"

"I know nothing about their fate. I swear it." He kissed her then, just as he used to, kissed her till she longed for more and she felt the familiar throbbing deep down inside. "I meant what I said last time we met. I do love you so, more than I ever thought possible."

She held him tight. She had so many questions, but they could wait. For now she just wanted to hold him, she could not believe he was here, his arms around her, telling her he loved her. She had longed for those words for years and she had not believed them when she heard them in that filthy cell. She thought he was just trying to make her feel better, perhaps to appease his conscience.

But there was one more thing she needed to know.

"Rosemary," she said.

"What about her?"

"Did you kill her?"

"Have you been wondering about her all this time? What do you think? Do you think I am capable of such a thing?"

"Yes," she replied. "I know you are quite capable of murder if it suits your purpose. And Anthony believes you killed her."

"Does he? Really? I didn't realise he even noticed she was gone."

"But you are capable of murder?"

"You are thinking of Connie's useless and violent husband?" He asked. She nodded. "He needed killing. Scum like him should not be allowed to live. But Rosemary was innocent; that was half her trouble. In truth, I suppose I did kill her in a way. It was my fault she killed herself," he replied at last. She frowned at him. "Rosemary committed suicide."

"But she is in your family crypt, beneath the church."

"Yes she is. I did little enough for her while she lived, the least I could do was be sure she was not cast out by the church she loved so much. She should have been a nun; she would have been happy with that, a bride of Christ. She should never have been forced into marriage." He paused and sighed despondently. "I found her body hanging over the bed in the east wing. That is why it was closed up. I took her to London, where I knew there was an outbreak of plague, where Anthony's parents had recently died of it. Nobody knew, nobody questioned and she could have her place in the family crypt."

"That was a nice thing to do," she said.

"It was the only good thing I ever did for her." His eyes met Bethany's. "I wish I could have done more for Rosemary, but I was young and arrogant and impatient. I'll not make that mistake again. You and I, we must share our deepest thoughts, there must be no more misunderstandings." He paused, as though trying to find the courage to go on. "That night in the cottage," he began, but she put her fingers up to his lips to halt his words.

"None of that matters," she said. "It is over now."

"No. You must let me tell you or I will never be able to live with myself." He took a deep breath and carried on. "That night I came home to see you, you thought someone had found you out, but you were wrong. I had felt bad since Anthony sent word that you knew about Rachel. I guessed what you must have been thinking and I thought at first it would be a good thing, it would make you think less of me. But I began to miss you too much. I wanted to try to explain, wanted you to know the truth. And I really wanted to see you, wanted to hold you in my arms, to feel the love that only you could give me. I had missed you so much and I gave in to my own weakness. You taught me that lust is not love; lust I could have any time."

She felt herself flinch. Did she want to know how far Lady Rachel's services had gone?

"Imagine my surprise to find your bed empty and no sign of you in the house. But while I searched I saw a light among the trees, so I went through the underground passage to the church. While you were arranging the departure of all those people, I was in the crypt, listening to every word."

She gasped, bit her lip.

"No wonder you were so angry."

"I was angry, and disappointed. I had ridden all this way to feel you in my arms, and I was angry with you and with myself. I believed I must have succeeded in my scheme to push you away. I thought I'd destroyed your love, for you to betray me like that and that it was too late to explain about Rachel.

"While I listened in the crypt, it gradually became clear that you were using my Summerville to help my enemies. God in Heaven! But I wanted to kill you then. I don't know how I kept myself under control." He paused and swallowed hard before he carried on. "I made my plan on the spur of the moment, but when I brought the carriage and took you back to the cottage, I had spent those hours letting it fester in my mind, wanting revenge for your betrayal. And when you struck me, I could barely contain my temper. I wanted to punish you."

"Do not speak of it. You did nothing you were not entitled to do."

"I think you know I don't believe that. Physical love between a man and a woman is something precious and beautiful; it should not be used as a weapon, it should never be used to hurt. I am very ashamed of my actions that night. I only want to know you forgive me, that it'll not ruin our future."

Future. Did that mean they had a future, a future together?

"When I volunteered to help Charles Carlisle," she said, "it never occurred to me that I would be betraying you and your beliefs. I did it for Julia, and because I knew I had already lost you." She captured an escaping sob. "You said you would kill me. I was terrified you would carry out your threat, I was afraid of every strange noise."

He pulled her close to him again and there were tears in his eyes.

"I would never have lived with myself had I hurt you and I would not have carried out my threat, not once I was calmer. I know two people found you, one who knew your identity and one who did not. But it seemed neither one could tempt you from your hiding place, so I was spared the dilemma of having to think about it."

"I am so sorry, Richard," she said. "I should never have made all those promises to you, not when I had no idea if I would be able to keep them."

"You broke every one of them," he said, but there was no anger in his tone. "Yet I cannot see how you could have done anything different. There is but one of the promises I fear you might have broken of your own free will."

"What?"

"I asked someone to follow Carlisle, to find out what he was doing. He followed him to the priest's cottage."

Her heart jumped.

"I did not invite him," she said. "He was curious. He wanted to take me away, to help me, nothing more, I swear it."

"And you refused to go with him?"

"Yes. I would not have left Alicia, but I would not have gone anyway. He was still helping

Protestants to escape and I was not brave enough to do that again."

"And that is all? That was the only time you saw him?"

"Of course. What are you talking about?"

"The man who was following him believed him to be your lover."

She stared at him in horror, studying his expression intently. Was he angry, jealous?

"Richard, I failed to give you a son, I failed to become a Catholic, I even failed to behave like the countess you made me, but I would never, ever be unfaithful to you. I could never do that; I love you too much and nobody will ever take your place in my bed or in my heart." She leaned forward and kissed him. "Do you believe me?"

She was relieved to see him smile.

"I believe you. Even when he suggested it, I could not believe it was true. Perhaps I am too conceited."

She kissed his cheek.

"What will you do now?" She asked reluctantly. "Will you find a place at the court of Queen Elizabeth?"

"I doubt it. She may have pardoned her sister's enemies, but she does not trust them. I betrayed Mary; she sees no reason why I wouldn't also betray her." He paused thoughtfully for a moment, then went on: "Besides, I do not believe I could tolerate being so close to a Protestant monarch."

"You still adhere to the Catholic faith? After everything Mary did, after all the horrific deaths, how can you?"

"It was a pure and simple faith, easy enough to follow, easy enough to believe. It gave comfort in confession and absolution." He stopped and hugged her closer. At last he went on. "I had great hopes when Mary became Queen. I believed she would convince the people that it was the right way, the true faith. I lost patience with her very early on and I was not the only one. She had the opportunity not only to bring England back to Catholicism, but to prove a woman could rule wisely. She threw away those opportunities and for that I cannot forgive her. Instead of bringing England back to the church of Rome, she has ensured that no Catholic will ever again sit securely on the throne of England." His jaw clenched as he went on bitterly: "She has turned the communion wine into holy poison."

"I am sorry," Bethany whispered. "I am sorry you were disappointed with your Queen and I am more sorry that I could not follow you, that I could not keep my promises." She hugged him tighter, hoping to make him understand, even though she did not really understand herself. She wanted to do something for him, something to ease his disenchantment. "It all seemed so easy at the time. All I had to do was change my faith to one I believed was dead and gone and meant nothing, tolerate your infidelities and give you a son. I failed in all of those things, failed miserably. I am so very sorry."

"It was my own fault," he said swiftly. "I was attracted to you because you could not pretend, because of your openness and honesty, and I was arrogant enough to believe your faith was unimportant, not the true faith. I believed you would soon see that. How could I have expected you to follow me?"

"Can we stay here, together, at Summerville, where we were happy? It is not yet too late to have a son; you will give me a chance to keep that promise?"

"I would like that," he said quietly. "I would like to start again, if that is possible, if you can put the past years away, out of your mind. I know you once loved me. I would give anything to know I've not completely destroyed that love. Could we start again? Or is it too late?"

Her lips found his and kissed him with all the passion and longing she had carefully held in check for the past four years and her heart sang when she felt his body stir in response.

"Does that answer your question, My Lord?"

"Richard," he replied. "My name is Richard."

THE END

Author's Note: Thank you for reading Holy Poison: The Judas Pledge. I hope you have enjoyed it and if you have, please leave a review on the Amazon website.

Don't miss the other five books in the series.

Please consider my other books:

The Romany Princess
The Gorston Widow
The Crusader's Widow
The Wronged Wife
To Catch a Demon
The Adulteress
Conquest
The Loves of the Lionheart
The Cavalier's Pact
The Minstrel's Lady (winner of 2017 e festival of words Best Romance)
A Man in Mourning

Pestilence Series:

The Second Wife
The Scent of Roses
Once Loved (winner 2017 e festival of words Best Historical)

The Elizabethans:

The Earl's Jealousy
The Viscount's Divorce
Lord John's Folly

The Hartleighs of Somersham

A Match of Honour
Lady Penelope's Frenchman

Non-historical

Old Fashioned Values
Mirielle

If you want to receive notification of future publications, as well as some free books, http://www.historical-romance-readers.com

Made in the USA
Columbia, SC
01 November 2020

23815298R00178